AF010981

THE SECRET OF
GALLOWAY'S STONES

First published 2024

Copyright © Jahc Leneveu 2024

The right of Jahc Leneveu to be identified as the author of this work has been asserted in accordance with the Copyright, Designs & Patents Act 1988.

All rights reserved. No part of this book may be reproduced, stored in a retrieval system, or transmitted in any form or by any means, digital, electronic, electrostatic, magnetic tape, mechanical, photocopying, recording or otherwise, without the written permission of the copyright holder.

Published under licence by Brown Dog Books and
The Self-Publishing Partnership Ltd, 10b Greenway Farm, Bath Rd, Wick, nr. Bath BS30 5RL, UK

www.selfpublishingpartnership.co.uk

ISBN printed book: 978-1-83952-811-8
ISBN e-book: 978-1-83952-812-5

Cover design by Andrew Prescott
Internal design by Andrew Easton

Printed and bound in the UK

This book is printed on FSC® certified paper

The Secret of Galloway's Stones

Jahc Leneueu

-1-

Have you ever noticed how strange things seem to happen out of nothing? How the smallest and most insignificant things people say or do can lead to an avalanche of problems that soon get out of control? Well, I call this phenomenon 'The Snowball Effect'. Like an avalanche, it's fast, unpredictable and can be triggered at any time. Take me, for example. My 'snowball' started rolling three months ago, on a regular Friday morning, just after Mum received a simple phone call from her sister Aunt Cecilia.

'Guess what?' Mum said after putting the phone down. 'Cecilia is having a conservatory built.'

'Oh, yeah …' Dad said casually over his morning paper.

'It's not any kind of conservatory,' she continued. 'It's a Victorian conservatory with a glass cupola and roof lanterns. Richard is going to landscape the garden while he's at it. From what Cecilia was saying, it's going to look amazing once it's finished!' Mum announced triumphantly.

'Is Richard *actually* going to do the job himself or is he going to get a contractor to do the hard work and take all the credit for himself *as per usual*?' said Dad, finally lifting his nose from his paper.

Dad doesn't care much for Uncle Richard; he always says that he's *'an arrogant pompous .... BEEP...!'* (I'm not allowed to use that word as it is a bit rude, you see. But let's just say that if Mrs James, my mathematics teacher caught me using that word she would put me on detention for the rest of the term, if not the rest of the year!) Me on the other hand, I don't mind Uncle Richard; he's always been nice to me. He always remembers my birthday, and every time he sees me he gives me some pocket money.

Of course, Uncle Richard dresses a bit weird, always in his tweed trousers at weekends and in his neatly pressed pin-striped suits during the week, but that has to come with the job, right? He works in the City, in one of those tall fancy buildings overlooking London. He's got his very own office on the top floor and apparently the view from it is breathtaking. He's some kind of banker or something. Mum always says that Uncle Richard is 'quite high-up', to which Dad always answers, 'Up his own ...!' (*BEEP* again. It's the same word that I can't use for punishment reasons.)

Dad and Uncle Richard could not be any more different if they tried. My dad works the night shift in a post office, and while Uncle Richard goes to work in his brand-spanking-new top-of-the-range BMW convertible, Dad goes to work on his push bike. They have different tastes and views on everything, you name it ... But if I had to sum them up, I'd have to say that Dad likes football and beer, and Uncle Richard likes cricket and Pimm's ... Once you've got that, you've understood everything.

Nan told me one day – and I have to admit that I find it hard to believe – that Uncle Richard and Dad used to be best friends at college, just before they met my mum. According to Nan, they both used to fancy my mum, but when she chose Dad over Uncle Richard, the boys fell out. Apparently, Uncle Richard was so heartbroken that he accepted a scholarship to Oxford University to be as far away as possible from Mum. There, he studied business, got an 'MBA' or something and this is how he landed his great job in London. My dad stayed in Palnure, unsure if he wanted to pursue a career in sport or music. In the end, he took a summer job at the post office and ended up staying there.

Nan's story goes that one day, as Uncle Richard was visiting his parents in Dumfries, he bumped into my mum's younger sister, Cecilia. They chatted for a while, went for a drink and then had dinner, and I suppose this is how they fell in love. Uncle Richard and Aunt Cecilia had a fairy-tale wedding in Ireland in front of hundreds of people and went on a cruise around the Caribbean islands for their honeymoon. My mum and dad got married in Palnure's register office, and for their honeymoon they spent two nights in a B&B in the Lake District. Uncle Richard and Aunt Cecilia live in Richmond upon Thames in England, in a three-storey house overlooking the river, and we live in a tiny cottage on the edge of Palnure in Scotland. I have younger twin sisters, Samantha and Rebecca, who are ten, and Uncle Richard and Aunt Cecilia have only one son, William, who is a year younger than me. I go to St Margaret's comprehensive school and my cousin William goes to Eton College near Windsor. I could carry on for hours, listing the differences in our lives but I am going to stop right here as I think you've got the picture.

I've often wondered what my life would be like if my mum had married Uncle Richard instead of my dad. Would I have a sleek haircut like my cousin William instead of my funky spiky hair? Would I wear neatly pressed polo shirts instead of my creased baggy T-shirts? Who knows? We are not rich, but to tell you the truth I think I would rather be in my old trainers than in my cousin William's nicely polished shoes any time.

'You're missing the point, *Jonathan*,' continued Mum, still going on about the Victorian conservatory.

'And what is the point, exactly *Diane*?' said Dad, finally putting his paper down.

I've noticed that it's never a good sign when Mum and Dad start calling each other by their first name. A 'Diane' here and a 'Jonathan' there is always sign of troubles ahead ...

'The point is, that *my* sister, is going to have a fantastic-looking garden and all I've got is an overgrown lawn full of weeds and some very wonky slabs for a terrace!' Mum added rather loudly, pointing at our tired looking back garden.

'It just needs a bit of trimming and weeding. That's all,' said Dad shrugging his shoulders looking out the window.

'Not this time, *Jonathan*,' snapped Mum. 'It will need more than TLC!'

'And what have you actually got in mind, *Diane*?'

'I think it's time for our garden to get a makeover …'

'A makeover? Shall we call Alan Titchmarsh and Charlie Dimmock?' Dad said sarcastically.

I love my mum to bits, but she watches far too many DIY programmes if you ask me. I remember last year when she decided it was time to 'update' our bathroom. Dad – who is not the best DIY expert around – bodged the job, so now we have to dodge falling tiles every time we take a shower. I don't know what he did to the plumbing, either, but there is now hardly any pressure. Our shower has to be the worst in Scotland as it lets out a tiny drizzle of water at a time and it takes forever to rinse out the shampoo from your hair.

'Decking would look nice,' Mum carried on, ignoring Dad's sarcastic comments. 'And I would love a pergola and a pond too …'

'Your wish is my command, my Lady,' said Dad, taking a bow, pretending to be a medieval knight. 'You shall have your fancy *decking, pergola and pond!*' he added, kissing Mum on the cheek. 'Jake and I will start tomorrow. Hey, boy, how do you fancy helping your old dad?' he asked, winking at me.

I couldn't think of anything worse than spending a whole weekend digging up the garden but 'us boys' stick together, so I said 'Sure! You're on!' in my most excited pretend voice.

So, on Saturday, Dad and I went to the local DIY shop. We spent ages walking through the aisles comparing prices and filling our trolley with strange-looking tools. We then queued for hours at the till (of course DIY shops are very busy on Bank Holiday weekends) and we spent even longer trying to load everything safely onto the roof of our old Peugeot 306 estate. By the time we arrived home, offloaded everything into the garden and grabbed a quick sandwich, it was already two o'clock.

Dad had come up with a plan of action. He was to do all the 'hard graft' as he likes to call it and I was going to be his assistant. It basically means that he trashes and demolishes everything in his path, and I am left to follow behind him, picking up the mess. We worked nonstop till eight o'clock that evening. I was starved and exhausted. I went to bed just before nine and when I woke up on Sunday, I was aching from head to toe.

'What do you reckon?' asked Dad as soon as I stepped foot into the garden. 'It looks much better already, doesn't it?'

'Much better,' I said, trying to sound convincing. The truth was that the garden was a state. It looked like World War Three had started in it overnight! There was rubble and heaps of rubbish lying all around. The skip was full of stuff and the smoke from the bonfire Dad had lit to burn some of the rubbish was stinging my eyes like mad.

'Ready?' Dad asked me.

I said *'YES'* because I had to, not feeling too thrilled about spending another day in the garden. We dug the hole for Mum's pond for what felt like hours. I don't know how deep Dad intended to dig, but he was about waist deep when I heard a hollow *THUD*. Dad had hit something.

'Stupid pickaxe! It's stuck. Jake, pass me the shovel, please.' He added angrily, snapping his fingers at me.

I did as I was told and took a few steps back. It's better to keep your distance with Dad when things don't go his way, since he has a tendency of losing his rag very fast. Things were not looking too good as the pickaxe was still stuck in whatever it was stuck in. Dad was getting redder and redder in the face by the minute with heat, anger or both – I was not too sure – and huge beads of sweat were pouring down his face. I watched him for a while, fighting with the shovel and the pickaxe when suddenly I noticed his red face turning into a very strange shade of white-green.

'AAH!' he suddenly screamed like Mum when she sees a spider, and jumping out of the hole and dropping his pickaxe and shovel at the same time, he shouted at me, 'Jake! Call the police! There's a body buried in our back garden!'

-2-

It turned out that the 'body' found in our back garden was not 'a gruesome discovery' like everybody thought at first, but 'the discovery of the century'. According to a team of archaeologists and anthropologists who have taken residence in our back garden, we have the best preserved 'Celtic Iron Age Bog Mummy' in the world! Mum is relieved that we have not bought the house of a mass murderer and Dad is over the moon as he has got one over on Uncle Richard.

'Well *Richard* may have a fancy "Victorian conservatory" in his back garden but *WE* have a *MUMMY* in *OURS*!' was the only thing on Dad's lips.

The week that followed the discovery of the Mummy, my mum and dad, my sisters and I, became kind-of celebrities. We had our photo printed on the front of *The Daily Gazette* and our interview was spread over three pages. It was funny to read how my dad 'always knew there was something special about our house' and 'how a special force had made him dig the hole'. Nevertheless, it was an amazing week. Dad was given the key to the town by Mayor Turner for putting Palnure on the map. We had neighbours and members of the public hanging off our fences, trying to get a glance of the

Mummy. We had people phoning from all over the world to confirm the rumours and we even had the *Time Team* TV crew turning up for a special recording on the 'Bog Mummy'. It was brilliant! `

At school, I was propelled from obscurity to stardom overnight. Geri – the prettiest girl in school and probably the whole of Scotland – started talking to me. Of course, her ex-boyfriend Alan was not too happy, but what could he do about it? He may have had a very promising future as a Scottish professional football player but I was the cool kid with a Mummy in his back garden. People I had never spoken to kept saying 'Hi' to me and I was bombarded with questions and surrounded on my every break at school. Older kids kept patting me on the shoulders saying, 'Cool one, Jake,' and I was loving every second of it. Even my teacher Mrs James was nice to me. She had allowed me to have a few afternoons off, as long as I did a presentation on 'the Mummy in my back garden.'

I didn't mind doing a presentation on the subject because it was not like real schoolwork. I have learned so much about the life of Celtic people in the Iron Age and about the land surrounding us. Two thousand years ago, the whole area where our neighbourhood now stands was an ancient marsh land, a giant swamp if you like. It's funny to think that just walking down our high street in those days would have been very difficult and very smelly! Tom, the head of the archaeologists, told me that the man buried in our garden was most probably a druid, judging by some of the artefacts buried with him. He had also let me name the Mummy. I first wanted to call him Scott, as we are in Scotland, but in the end I decided to call him 'Galloway' after the County we live in.

I find archaeology interesting, and I wouldn't mind being an archaeologist when I am older. It's kind of cool. It's not your boring Monday-to-Friday, nine-to-five kind of job. You travel the world, you play with cool tools and you get to wear combat trousers. I've also noticed that it is a 'girl-magnet', as since the discovery of Galloway, Geri had taken the habit of walking back from school with me every day. The Friday afternoon following the discovery of the Mummy, I finally plucked up the courage to invite her in, and of course, of all the days to pick, I had to pick the day Mum was in a foul mood.

'It's impossible to keep this house clean when you've got people coming in and out of it as if it was Piccadilly Circus!' Mum shouted, as soon as we walked in. 'You two – take your shoes off,' she ordered us. It was hardly the welcome I had expected. But Geri didn't seem to mind and to my biggest surprise, she started complimenting my mum on our house and on 'how lovely it was arranged'. It seemed to work, as Mum managed to crack a smile and offered us some drinks. Dad, on the other hand, was over the moon. He couldn't stop smiling and winking at me, putting his thumbs up, mumbling 'well done, Jake – pretty girl', behind Geri's back. I was furious and terribly embarrassed as he was hardly subtle. I really hoped Geri had not noticed my dad's embarrassing and immature behaviour. Sometimes I wonder who is twelve years old – him or me? Fortunately for me, Geri was far too interested and excited by what was happening in the back garden to pay any notice to my dad. Tom had just finished briefing his team and I seized this opportunity to introduce him to Geri and run away from Dad.

'Do you want to go to my room?' I asked Geri once Tom had answered all her questions. 'My bedroom is in the attic, and you've got a good view of the whole garden from up there.'

I had carefully planned my invitation. I had spent hours the day before, carefully tidying my room, picking up my dirty clothes off the floor and getting rid of my old Action Man figures and my motorbike posters that were covering the walls. I thought the result was a total success as I didn't even recognise my own bedroom.

'So, you are telling me that you haven't sneaked under that tent to see what the Mummy looks like?' Geri said in disbelief, looking out of my bedroom window.

'Well, yeah, we're not allowed.' I said, realising too late how stupid I must have sounded.

'Jake Fagan, I didn't know you were such a goody two shoes,' she said smiling. 'Do you always do as you are told?'

'No!' I protested too quickly to sound sincere. 'It's just that we can't go in the tent. It is always full of people. Look for yourself,' I said, pointing at the half-dozen archaeologists under my window. 'They have so much to do. They have to map the area, take photos, collect data and ...'

'Sounds boring to me,' she said, interrupting me. 'When are they moving the body?'

'Sometime next week ... I think ...' I said, a bit surprised by her question.

'Good! That still leaves us with a few days to go and investigate inside the tent to see what Galloway looks like,' she said with a sparkle in her eyes. 'When can we go?'

'What do you mean?' I said, a bit confused.

'*When ... can ... we ... go ... and ... see ... the ... mummy?*' she repeated slowly and loudly as if I was hard of hearing.

'I told you we can't. It's always full of people during the day.'

'Then we'll have to go at night!' she declared very matter of fact.

'At night?' I asked surprised and a bit shocked.

'Well, yeah, it does make sense,' she said, hands on her hips. 'If we can't go during the day then we'll have to go at night. Don't tell me you're scared?'

'No, I am not!' I said on the defensive.

'Then that's sorted. We shall go tonight!' she declared triumphally.

I had fallen for it. Geri had me exactly where she wanted me. I couldn't say 'No' as she would have thought that I was a coward and would have most probably told everybody about it. I was doomed if I did and doomed if I didn't. It was brilliant – pure genius from her part! Girls are far cleverer than us boys.

'I'll see you tonight, then,' she said. 'Wear dark clothes so that no one spots us and don't forget a torch. I'll bring my Dad's Swiss Army Knife, just in case ...'

I couldn't believe that she had already worked out a plan of action, so I said 'OK,' trying to regain some control over the situation. 'I'll meet you by the front gate at midnight. The back gate is rusty and very noisy. We'll wake my mum up if we try to open it.'

'You're a star!' she said, giving me a big hug.

I remember mumbling something stupid like, 'Okey dokey ... See you tonight ...' blushing from head to toe before realising what I had just agreed to ...

* * *

Geri was outside my front gate at midnight on the dot. She was wearing a black pair of skinny jeans, a black long-sleeved T-shirt, a black cap and she had even put some black make-up on her face like they do in the army to be undetectable by the enemy. I suddenly felt very underdressed in my tracksuit bottoms and sweatshirt, so I quickly put my hood up to look the part.

'Have you got the torch?' she asked.

'Yeah,' I whispered. Good job I had the sense to check the batteries earlier on, otherwise I would have looked like a complete idiot. The batteries were dead and the only replacements I could find came from the TV remote control. Dad was not going to be too happy to find that his best friend 'the remote' had passed away during the night ...

'Good,' she smiled. 'Then lead the way...'

Our garden looked very creepy under the full moon's light. It was just like a scene from a horror movie where you would expect to come face to face with a zombie. Mum's unkempt and overgrown rose bushes were casting strange shadows onto our lawn and the wind that was softly blowing against our broken fence was making a strange hissing noise. I really started to regret listening to Geri. I felt sick in my stomach, and I had the horrible feeling that being there was a bad idea, a very bad idea ...

'Are you sure you want to do this?' I said, stopping in front of the white tent where the Mummy laid.

'Positive!' she answered.

It was too late to change my mind. I had to get on with it, even though every inch of my body was telling me to walk away now. I slowly lifted the side panel of the tent, took a deep breath and stepped inside ...

-3-

The inside of the tent looked like a scene from a murder investigation. There were white lab coats and hazmat suits hanging on racks; boxes of gloves, face masks and goggles were stacked up on top of each other. There was high-tech looking equipment piled up high onto tables and strange-looking markings on the floor.

'Watch where you step,' I said to Geri, pointing at an area that had been cornered off by some red-and-white tape. 'We mustn't leave any sign of us being here so please do not touch anything, and try to be quiet. The last thing we want is being caught red-handed in here by my mum. We'll be in for the punishment of the century!' I could tell by Geri's body language that she was not listening to me. She was like a kid who had just stepped into the best sweet shop in the world.

'Is that him over there?' she asked with excitement, pointing at a tarpaulin in the middle of the tent.

'I guess so ...' I said stretching my neck to see.

'Cool! Let's see what he looks like,' she said, clapping her hands together.

'No!' I said. 'We are not allowed to touch anything! We could contaminate the site by accident!'

'Jake,' Geri started. 'If you think I've come all this way at this time of the night without even taking a peek at the Mummy, then you've got another thing coming!' She said, whipping the tarpaulin off.

I don't know what I was expecting but Galloway didn't look anything like I had imagined. He was lying on his back, eyes closed, his head slightly tilted to the side as if asleep. Only his upper body was visible, the rest of him was still unearthed.

'WOW!' exclaimed Geri. 'Look at that! You can still see his ginger hair and beard! And his skin looks like brown leather!'

'That's normal,' I said, remembering something Tom had told me. 'It's the acidity of the ground that gives the skin and hair its colouring. The bog has some special chemical properties that prevent bodies from deteriorating.'

'Very impressive, Mr Fagan,' said Geri. 'Not just a pretty face, hey …' she added smiling at me. 'Come on, don't stand there doing nothing. Take a photo of me with Galloway,' she said, handing me over her mobile phone.

I was about to protest when suddenly Max, the dog from next door, starting barking.

'What's going on, boy?' I heard the deep voice of Mr Anderson from his bedroom window. Instinctively, I had put my hand on Geri's mouth to keep her quiet and quickly turned the torch off.

'What is it, Angus?' I heard Mrs Anderson ask her husband.

'Probably nothing,' he said grumpily 'Max must have seen a cat or something ...'

Geri and I waited for a little while, crouching motionless in the dark, patiently waiting for the coast to clear before talking.

'That was close,' she said.

'Too close,' I said, turning the torch back on. 'Come on. Let's go'

'Wait!' Geri ordered. 'What's that?' she said, pointing at something by Galloway's waist. 'Something is glittering ...'

'I don't know, and I don't care! Let's go now before Max starts barking again!'

'Just a second,' she said ignoring me. 'I just want to check what it is before we go. Hold the torch for me, please.'

I did as I was told, far too tired to argue. I had already had enough excitement for one night and all I wanted was to leave before being caught.

'You'll want to take a look at this,' she suddenly said. 'I think I've found something ... Something that your friend Tom and his team of "scientists" have missed!' she added with a smile on her face.

She was right. Something was shining by Galloway's side.

'What is it?' she said, as I bent down to examine her find.

'I'm not too sure. It looks like a tiny buckle ... or a brooch ... something like that. I can see why Tom has missed it, though – it only glitters when the light of the torch touches it,' I said, turning the light on and off it a few times to show her. 'It seems to be attached to something.'

'Well, whatever it is, it's mine. Finders keepers!' Geri said a bit too loud. Her outburst had echoed into the night and Max next door had instantly resumed his barking.

'Come on, let's go!' I said. 'We're going to get caught!'

'Not without MY discovery!' Geri said, refusing to move.

'We can't take it! Tom will see that Galloway has been touched.'

'I don't care! I am not going anywhere without what is *rightfully* mine!' Geri added, stumping her foot.

'What now, boy?' growled Mr Anderson from his window. 'I'm coming down!'

We didn't have much time as Mr Anderson was closing in. So I quickly picked up Geri's find, shoved it in my pocket, grabbed her by the hand and ran out of the tent.

* * *

'Show me what it is!' Geri said, once we were both in the safety of my bedroom.

I plunged my hand in my pocket and took out of it a brown leathery-looking pouch, about the size of a peach. It was tied off with a platted lace and two tiny buckles were dangling out of both ends.

'A purse!?' exclaimed Geri. 'What do you think it contains?' Her eyes were like two embers, shinning with excitement. 'Coins? Gold? Diamonds?' she carried on.

I was as eager as her to find out what was in the pouch so, unable to wait any longer, I started opening it. It was not easy, trying to undo a 2000-year-old knot, but slowly and surely, I managed to loosen it up enough to tip its contents out. Four brown stones had fallen out of it and rolled into the palm of my hand.

'Stones?' said Geri. 'Is that all?' she added disappointingly, snatching the pouch out of my hand and shaking it to make sure that nothing was left inside. 'All that for nothing?'

'Well not for nothing,' I said sheepishly. 'We saw Galloway, so surely that has to count for something?'

'I suppose you're right,' she said. 'I would have preferred finding precious stones, though,' she added with a mischievous smile. 'It's late. I'd better go.' She looked at her watch. 'You can keep Galloway's stones, they're yours. I think you deserve them. And I think you deserve this too ...' she added, before kissing me quickly on the lips.

It was almost daylight by the time I managed to fall asleep. I heard Dad coming back from his night shift at the post office. I was exhausted but far too hyper to sleep. Last night's events kept playing at the back of my mind. We had seen Galloway, but even better, Geri had kissed me! I was lying in bed, restless, worried out of my mind that Tom would find out I had been in the tent. I was nervously playing with the stones, rolling them in the palm of my hand – they were smooth and very soothing.

'I really hope no one finds out we've been in the tent,' I said to myself, yawning. I was past exhaustion, and I could feel my eyelids getting heavier and heavier. I put the stones back in their pouch and placed them carefully under my pillow. The last thing I remember was closing my eyes. But as I did so, I could have sworn I saw a purple spark…

-4-

An annoying chant of '*Jake! Jake! Jake!*' woke me up on Saturday morning. And what can be more annoying than your little sister trying to wake you up when you have had hardly any sleep? I'm going to tell you what. Two sisters! I don't know how twins do it, but they've got a natural ability for being doubly annoying as everything they say or do is perfectly timed and synched.

'Go away!' I said, pulling the cover over my head. 'I'm tired and not in the mood for the two of you! Leave me alone and let me sleep!'

I don't care what Mum says, but Dad must have the patience of a saint to be able to put up with the twins on a daily basis after a night shift. I only had a few hours' sleep and I felt terribly grumpy. I had tightly wrapped the duvet around me like a cocoon, to muffle their shouts, but the twins, who were on a mission to wake me up, were not going to be discouraged so easily. They had climbed onto my bed and were jumping up and down in a perfectly synchronised bounce that was sending me flying a foot high in the air. I could say goodbye to my lie-in…

'Stop it!' I ordered them. 'I feel sick!'

'Jake! Come on!' They said in unison, ignoring my request. 'Everybody is waiting for you!'

'Who is everybody?' I asked grumpily from the inside of my cocoon.

'Tom and his team, for a start ... Mum and Dad and ... *your girlfriend, Geri!*' they added in a giggle.

'And why would they be waiting for me?'

'Because Galloway is being moved! That's why!'

'What?!' I suddenly screamed in disbelief. I don't think I could have jumped out of bed faster if the twins had tipped a bucket of ice-cold water on my head. The news of Galloway's sudden departure had sent adrenaline rushing through my body like an electric wave. I was suddenly wide awake, and as I had fallen asleep fully dressed I was downstairs in a matter of seconds and Mum, of course, couldn't resist commenting on it.

'That was quick!' she said with a smile. 'If only you could get out of bed that fast on school days!'

'Here you are!' said Tom as soon as he saw me. 'You're just in time. We're about to move Galloway.'

'Why?' I asked in a panic. 'Why so fast? I mean, is something wrong? I was scared that Tom had decided to move Galloway because he had found out I went in the tent the night before.

'No, everything is fine,' said Tom. 'The equipment we needed to move Galloway turned up unexpectedly this morning. So, it means that we can now move him safely in one piece. The sooner we get him out, the sooner your life can get back to normal,' he added, pointing at a growing crowd hanging off our fences. 'Galloway should be on his way to Glasgow University this evening. Wish us good luck, we're about to start...'

'Nice hair!' I heard a sarcastic voice behind me once Tom had left.

It was Geri.

'What are you doing here?' I said, running a hand through my hair. I had got out of bed so fast that I had not put gel in my hair, and as a result it was as flat as a pancake.

'Oh dear... Has someone got up on the wrong side of the bed this morning?' Geri asked with a smile.

'Sorry, I didn't mean to snap at you. It's just that I was not expecting all of this ...' I said, looking around me. At least a dozen people were whizzing past us, hurrying in every direction.

'How long have you been here for?' I asked her.

'About fifteen minutes ...' she said, looking at her watch. 'And...' she added. 'Before you ask, no one knows we've been in the tent. Our nocturnal expedition has gone unnoticed. So stop worrying and start enjoying yourself. It's not every day that you get a front-row seat to the removal of a two-thousand-year-old Mummy, is it?'

I don't think Geri realised how relieved I was to hear that we had got away with it. Her news had instantly lifted my spirit and I felt on top of the world. Mum and Dad, the twins, Geri and I spent an amazing day together, chatting and joking in the sun while Tom and his team were hard at work. It was slow and backbreaking work, as the block of peat containing Galloway had to be carefully cut by hand with bog shovels in order to free him. Six hours later, in the presence of several archaeologists, biologists and paleobotanists, he was ready to embark on the next phase of his journey. I was a bit sad to see him go as I had got used to having him around. I think that Geri had guessed I was a bit upset because she asked me to walk her home. We had not gone as far as the phone box down the road, when I heard someone shout my name.

'Hey! Fagan! You little weed!' It was Alan, Geri's ex-boyfriend. 'What are you doing with my girl?' He looked so angry that I am pretty sure my nose would have been introduced to his right fist if it were not for Geri stepping between us.

'Alan! Go away!' she ordered him. 'And how many times do I have to tell you? I am not YOUR girl!'

'Oh, I see, Fagan!' Alan shouted at me. 'You get a *girl* to protect you! You pathetic loser! It's about time that someone teaches you a lesson Mr *'I've got a Mummy in My Back Garden,'* he said menacingly cracking his knuckles. 'We need to settle this, you and I. Man to man. Once and for all. Tomorrow three o'clock behind the church,' he added spitting on the floor. 'And don't be late or else!' And with that he left, gesturing a very rude sign in my direction.

'What has just happened?' I said. 'Have I just agreed to fight Alan?'

* * *

For the second night in a row, I was lying in bed, restless. I was tossing and turning, unable to get comfortable, when suddenly I felt a bulge under my pillow. It was Galloway's stones, and with the day's excitements I had completely forgotten about them. As I got them out of their pouch, I noticed that one of them was cracked.

'Good one, Jake!' I snapped angrily at myself. 'Two thousand years in the ground and they're intact. Twenty-four hours in your possession and they are broken!'

As I was checking the cracked stone to see if I could fix it with superglue or something, I suddenly realised that it was not actually broken. What I had taken for a crack was in fact some mud that had dried and come loose and the original colour of the stone was coming through. I was curious to see what they all looked like and as I couldn't sleep, so I decided to give the stones a good clean. I started by soaking them in lukewarm soapy water to soften the dry mud, then with a bit of elbow grease – and the help of Mum's flannel and Dad's toothbrush – half an hour later I had four colourful stones in my possession. I was amazed to see that two thousand years in the ground had not tarnished their colour and beauty. The red stone was still as red as a ripe cherry, the white stone was still as white as freshly fallen snow, the green stone was still as green as the grass of St Andrew's golf course and the blue stone was as blue as Geri's eyes ...

I was very pleased with my discovery but the prospect of

a fight with Alan was spoiling my mood. So, like the night before, unable to sleep, I was nervously stroking the stones as it was very comforting. I could not believe that in less than twelve hours I would have to fight someone twice my size. Alan is quite tall and muscular with all the football he plays and as for me – if I'm totally honest – I am quite small for my age. I am what Dad calls a 'slow bloomer'. While most of the boys in my class are starting to show signs of facial hair and a manly voice, I, on the other hand, show none of those attributes. Dad assures me that it 'will come in due time' and that I just 'need to be patient'. But that's easy for him to say – he's not the one with smooth rosy cheeks and a girly voice. Everybody in my family gets me confused with the twins over the phone. It has become such a complex of mine that I don't answer the phone anymore. The phone can ring and ring for hours and I will not pick it up.

'I really hope that Alan doesn't hurt me tomorrow …' I said before putting the stones back in their pouch. It took me forever to fall asleep that night and when I finally did, I might as well have not bothered as it was the worst sleep I ever had. I kept dreaming that Alan was chasing me … I was running after Galloway … And strange purple sparks were flying all around us …

-5-

The news of a fight between Alan and I had spread like a wild fire, and pretty much everybody from school was present. I had never seen the churchyard so busy. Father Glenn would have been very happy to have half that number turn up for his Sunday service.

'Look at all those people ...' I said to Geri. 'I don't even know half of them!'

'You don't have to fight Alan' Geri said. 'You can walk away now, you know.'

'And have Alan and his gang on my case for the rest of the year? I don't think so!'

'Boys ...' said Geri in a disapproving tone. 'You and your stupid pride ... I don't think I'll ever understand you!'

'Well, well – Fagan,' I heard the deep voice of Alan from behind me just as the clock struck three. 'I have to admit that I was not expecting to see you here. I didn't think he would have the bottle to turn up,' he said, turning to the growing crowd. 'He's either very brave or very stupid!' He laughed and everybody laughed with him. 'I hope you like the location. I chose it especially for you – quite fitting, wouldn't you say? The graveyard is just on the other side of the road. That way, we won't have to go too far to attend your funeral!' he added, and everybody doubled up with laughter. 'Come on, Fagan. Let's put you out your misery!' he snarled, fists clenched.

As I was standing motionless in front of Alan, ready to be used as a punching bag, I had a sudden déjà vu. I couldn't really explain why or how, but somehow I knew what was going to happen. So when Alan threw the first – and shall I say, the *only* – punch of the fight, I was ready for it and knew exactly what to do. I had ducked his right hook so fast, with the dexterity of a professional boxer, that my move had startled him. Alan punched through thin air, lost his balance and fell headfirst, flat on his nose. That was it for him. Game over …

* * *

Half an hour later, Geri and I were back in my bedroom, doing some maths revision for Monday's dreaded test. Maths has never been my favourite subject. I don't see the point to half these riddles and equations, especially not now that I've decided to become an archaeologist. *Irrational numbers...* They're all irrational to me if I'm being honest. *What is the square root of 275?* Who cares? The only root I'm interested in from now on is the root coming from a tooth or the root of a tree as they contain valuable archaeological information. And let me ask you – who decided to mix letters with numbers? I mean, does $x = \frac{-b \pm \sqrt{b^2 - 4ac}}{2a}$ make sense to you? Because it certainly doesn't to me. Letters and numbers don't go together. It's like putting gravy on your cereals – it's wrong!

I was pretending to read through Pythagoras's theorem but my mind was still on the fight. Well, if you can call that a fight ... It had been all over in seconds, a bit like last year Guy Fawkes fireworks display, come to think of it. What an anti-climax that day had been. It had been raining so much that day that some water managed to get to the powder so when they lit the fireworks, instead of taking off, they exploded on the spot in tiny fart-like pops here and there ...

I could see that Geri was finding it as hard as me to concentrate. She was holding her book on her chest, lying on my bed, staring at the ceiling.

'Do you think Alan's nose will ever stop bleeding?' she suddenly asked. 'Do you think it's broken?'

'I ... I don't know ...' I said. It was the truth. I never had a nosebleed in my life, let alone a broken nose.

We sat in silence for a while, reading through our notes, but after a couple of hours we decided to call it a day as it was pointless and nothing was sinking in. I was so tired that I went to bed after dinner without even watching TV, and like the night before, and the night before that, I was playing with Galloway's stones, slowly stroking them, amazed to see how quickly it had become a habit of mine before going to bed.

'I wish I didn't have to take that stupid maths test tomorrow ...' I said to myself before putting the stones back in their pouch. I was so tired that I fell asleep as soon as my head hit the pillow. Do you remember the story I told you about Guy Fawkes night and the fireworks? Well, I reckon it must have played on my mind because that night I dreamed of beautiful purple fireworks exploding in my bedroom ...

* * *

The whole school was in effervescence that Monday morning when I arrived at the gates. At first, I thought that everybody was talking about the 'fight' between Alan and I, but I soon realised that something else had taken centre stage ...

'Jake!' Geri shouted my name from the far end of the playground. 'The maths test is cancelled. Mrs James fell down the stairs and broke her leg.'

'What?!' I said, shocked at the news.

'You've just missed her. She's been taken to hospital by an ambulance.'

The news of Mrs James falling and hurting herself had unnerved me and even though it had nothing to do with me, I couldn't help but feel responsible. An unexplainable feeling of guilt stayed with me all day and it got me thinking ... What if Mrs James' accident was not an accident? After all, since the discovery of Galloway's stones, things had gone my way ... Geri and I had got away with being in the tent ... Alan had not hurt me ... And now the maths test had been cancelled ... What if the stones had something to do with it?

'Jake, you're being stupid now ...' I said to myself. 'It's just a coincidence ...' and I pushed the thought out of my mind.

But that night, as I was lying in bed with Galloway's stones in my hand, curiosity got the better of me. What if I was right? What if the stones *did have* something to do with the strange events that had taken place over the last few days?

I needed to know one way or another, so I decided to put the stones to the test. If I were to prove my theory right, I simply needed to wish for something before falling asleep. But what to wish for? It took me quite a while to decide what to wish for. There was so much I wanted. Mum and Dad are not rich and can't afford to buy us half the things we need. Don't get me wrong, we are not poor-poor, it's just that 'out of the ordinary' things are a real treat. Once Mum and Dad have paid the mortgage and all the bills, there is not much left for 'luxury' in the Fagan household and our things have to last us. Take my stereo, for example – it is Dad's old boombox. There is nothing wrong with it – it still works – but in terms of 'small and compact', well, I have seen better.

I went back and forth for a little while between a BMX and a tablet, and in the end I decided to go for the tablet.

'I wish I could have a tablet...' was the last thing I whispered before falling asleep ...

-6-

'Mum, your phone is ringing!' I shouted from the bottom of the stairs as I was about to leave for school.

'Pick it up please, honey – I'm busy,' Mum said from the bathroom.

I hate answering the phone, but since Mum was genuinely busy upstairs and I was only a few feet away from the phone, I picked it up.

'Hello,' I said in my most polite phone voice.

'Oh, good morning.' I heard the soft posh voice of Aunt Cecilia. 'This must be one of the twins. Rebecca or Samantha, which one are you? I can never tell you apart.'

'No, Aunt Cecilia. It's me. Jake.'

'Oh, I'm sorry, Jake, I thought it was one of your sisters.'

What did I tell you? Everybody gets me confused with the twins over the phone.

'It's OK, Aunt Cecilia', I said, pretending to be fine about the misunderstanding.

'Jake, while you're on the phone, let me wish you a happy birthday. I know your birthday is not until Friday, but I will not be able to phone on the day. Richard is whisking me away to Venice for a romantic weekend,' she said excitedly in a girly giggle. 'And since you are going to turn thirteen and officially become a teenager, your uncle and I have decided to send you a little surprise.'

'Thank you, Aunt Cecilia.' I said. 'You shouldn't have'.

'It's OK. Don't get too excited, it's nothing fancy. It's just a little something that we thought you might like.'

'Who is it?' Mum asked coming down the stairs, carrying the biggest pile of dirty clothes I had ever seen.

'Aunt Cecilia,' I said.

'Hi Cilia,' Mum said loudly so that Aunt Cecilia could hear her. 'Won't be a minute. Just need to chuck stuff in the washing machine and I'm all yours …'

'What are you up to?' Mum asked her sister once she had put the wash on. 'Wow…Venice…'

I could tell by the tone in Mum's voice that she would have given anything for just a glimpse of the Grand Canal, and that made me sad …

My day at school turned out to be one of those long tedious and boring days that never seemed to end. I couldn't concentrate on anything. Everything and everybody annoyed me, and to make matters worse, Geri, who had taken my silence for a sign of guilt over the 'Alan incident', was trying her best to cheer me up.

'Stop worrying,' she said as we were walking back home after school. 'I saw Alan this morning. He is OK. His nose is red and grazed. He'll survive. I think his pride hurts more than anything if you ask me. And I almost forgot … Mrs James is OK too. They expect a full recovery. She's got a cast, and she should be back at school in a couple of months. See you tomorrow,' she added before kissing me goodbye.

'This turned up for you early this afternoon,' Dad said to me as soon as I opened the front door. 'Stupid delivery guy woke me up,' he added grumpily, throwing the parcel at me. 'It's from your *aunt and uncle*,' he added with contempt.

I was holding my parcel at arm's length, speechless, too scared to open it. Anyone who was watching me now could have believed I was holding a dirty, smelly nappy that needed to be binned instead of a parcel.

'Give it here!' said Rebecca as she reached for my parcel. 'You're taking too long to open it!'

'No way!' said Samantha ripping the parcel open. 'A tablet!' she added enviously.

My present was the subject of the evening. Everybody loved it and was happy for me; that is everybody except for Dad, of course. He had not said a word and was quietly leaning against the fridge, a cup of coffee in his hands. I could tell by the way his lips curled that he didn't like my present one bit. It didn't really surprise me because anything that comes from Uncle Richard is just 'rubbish' in Dad's eyes.

That night, as I was lying in bed, staring in disbelief at the tablet on my bedside table and stroking Galloway's stones, I suddenly became very aware of the incredible power I was holding in my hands.

I was hyper, almost feverish. I needed to tell someone – I needed to tell Geri. After all, it was her discovery as much as it was mine. If it hadn't been for her decision to break into the tent we would never have found the stones. I was halfway through a text to Geri, telling her about Galloway's magical stones, when I suddenly stopped.

'But what if it is just a coincidence?' I thought to myself, feeling a bit stupid for the unnecessary agitation. After all, Uncle Richard and Aunt Cecilia always remember my birthday and send me a present every year. Moreover, they have money and love their technology. What is a tablet to them if not the perfect present to send their nephew?

The logical and rational side of my brain took over that night and I decided not to send Geri the text. As I was stroking Galloway's stones, laughing at my own stupidity, I suddenly remembered Aunt Cecilia's phone call and it triggered an old insecurity of mine. I've always hated my girly voice and my rosy pink cheeks, and being mistaken for one of the twins had been quite embarrassing.

'Now, if I could be "manlier", that would be real magic!' I laughed to myself, before falling asleep.

I woke up on Wednesday morning with far more than I had wished for. A full grown black wispy beard had sprouted overnight on my face! I couldn't believe how strange I looked. I didn't even recognise my own reflection in the mirror!

I couldn't let anyone see me as no one would ever believe that a twelve-year-old boy could suddenly grow such an impressive beard overnight, so I decided to get rid of it. I couldn't use Dad's electric shaver as it was far too noisy and it would draw attention to myself. So, I decided to use one of Mum's pink disposable razors – the one she uses to shave her legs – as it was a far more discreet option. I had filled the sink with lurk warm water and I caked my face with a complicated mixture of soap, bubble bath and shampoo because we didn't have any shaving foam. I dipped Mum's pink shaver in the water, wiggled it around and started shaving ...

Now, let me tell you a few things about shaving, and please, take my word for it. First thing, when you shave, do not use girl shavers. They are not designed for beards. They shred far more than they shave. I was covered with cuts, and I looked incredibly stupid with all the tiny pieces of toilet paper I had stuck to my face to stop the bleeding. Secondly, and probably most importantly, do not use aftershave. It stings and stinks like mad! That day, as I was walking to school with throbbing cheeks, it dawned on me that shaving was rubbish and I already hated it ...

* * *

'I don't know what to make of it all ...' Geri said once I had finished telling her my story about the stones and their secret. She had been silent all through my story, not interrupting me once, not even when I told her about me growing a full beard overnight! Her reaction was not at all what I had expected. Foolishly, I thought she was going to jump and scream with excitement, grab me by the neck and kiss me and ask me to lend her the stones. But to my biggest surprise, Geri was calm, quiet and pensive.

'We have to keep this for ourselves,' she suddenly said. 'No one must find out. Promise me, you won't say a word to anyone.'

'I promise ...' I said, crossing my heart. I was fine with keeping Galloway's stones and their power as our 'little' secret. Personally, I thought that the less people knew about them, the more wishes it was for us.

'And another thing, you can't make any more wishes, not until we understand more about the stones.'

'But ...' I started.

'No "but" Jake,' she interrupted me. 'It's extremely important. We must tread very carefully – we do not know what we are dealing with ... It could be dangerous. I need a few days to do some research. I'll go to the library, look on the internet, and I'll even go to the Aberdeen Museum if I have to. But please, Jake – no more wishes!' she added, suddenly very serious and stern looking.

'Alright,' I said, annoyed with her for forbidding me to use the stones. 'I won't make any more wishes. But I'm telling you one thing, you're wasting your time – no harm will ever come out of Galloway's stones!'

-7-

'HAPPY BIRTHDAY TO YOU … HAPPY BIRTHDAY TO YOU … HAPPY BIRTHDAY DEAR, JAKEY. HAPPY BIRTHDAY TO YOU!' Mum and the twins started singing as soon as I came back from school on Friday afternoon.

Mum had nicely decorated the house with balloons and banners for my birthday and a huge helium number 13 was floating in the living room. My birthday cards were all lined up on the mantel piece and the twins had pinned an 'I'm 13 today' badge on my chest.

'Time for your cake,' Mum said after dinner. She had baked a giant double-decker, triple chocolate-chip gateau, topped up with thirteen candles and two little sugar figurines representing a boy with spiky hair – me – and a man dressed all in white, holding a golden sickle – Galloway. Mum is very good at baking cakes and decorating them, so much so that people often ask her to bake cakes for special occasions like birthdays, weddings or christenings. I honestly think Mum could make a very nice living out of her cake baking if she could open her own business. But to have your own business you need money, and we don't have money …

'Make a wish!' the twins shouted as I was about to blow my candles. Last year, I would have jumped at the opportunity to make a wish, but this year I didn't need to. I had my own 'endless supply' of wishes, safely tucked under my pillow.

'Open Nan's present first,' Mum said, handing me a small parcel wrapped in blue paper. It was a model of a WWII Spitfire airplane. Bless Nan … She thinks I'm still into my toy 'models'. I noticed that she had left the price tag by accident at the bottom of the box. I didn't get offended when I saw the 'Reduced to Clear' £1 sticker. I know Nan's pension is not much …

'Cool!' I said. 'Remind me to phone Nan later on to thank her.'

'Ours now!' shouted the twins excitingly. They had gone to the computer game shop in town and had got me two 'pre-owned' fighting games that I had never heard of.

'Thanks, girls! I really wanted those two games,' I lied, trying to sound convincing.

'Now, for *'la piece de resistance'* Dad said with a smirk on his face, walking to the corner of the room. '*Et voila!*' he added proudly, whipping off a tired-looking blanket to reveal an even more tired-looking bike. 'Your very own BMX!'

I was frozen to the ground, in total shock, unable to move or talk at the 'unveiling' of my main birthday present. I don't think there is a word in the whole of the English vocabulary strong enough to describe my 'utter surprise'. If you add the words 'shock', 'stunned' and 'gobsmacked' together you're still a mile off my original reaction. For the first time in my life I was speechless, and Dad, who had taken my 'silence' for a good sign, was rubbing his hands together with utter contentment and excitement.

'Don't worry too much about the bowed front wheel, we can fix that easily. After a lick of paint and a few adjustments here and there your BMX will be as good as new! What did I tell you *Diane?* He likes his present! Good lad!' said Dad, patting me hard on the back. 'I tell you what, Jake, if you wake me up tomorrow afternoon we could fix your BMX and take it to the skate park for you to try a few tricks. What do you say?'

I still couldn't say anything as I had lost my talking abilities, but one thing was for sure, Dad could sleep all day tomorrow, I was not going to wake him up. There was no way I was going to take that rusty old piece of junk of a bike out; no way was I going to be seen alive riding that thing! I swear you could catch tetanus just by looking at it! If I didn't know Dad any better, I would have thought the whole thing was a wind-up. But sadly, it was not...

'Rock on, BMX!' Dad said, still rubbing his hands together excitingly. I wished he stop doing it because he reminded me of a fruit fly; like him, they are forever rubbing their two front legs together. 'And in your face, *Richard's Tablet!*'

I couldn't believe what I was hearing ... Who in their right mind would compare a brand-new tablet to an old rusty bike that looked that it had been rescued from a skip?

* * *

Later that evening, as I retreated to my bedroom on the pretence of wanted to play my new computer game, I came to a terrible realisation – it had been my worst birthday ever. I was pacing up and down my tired old brown carpet with a mixture of disappointment and resentment. I hated my 'reduced to clear' and 'pre-owned' presents. I hated my stupid, horrible, nasty bike. But more importantly, I hated my life! What was there to love? A quick glance around my room was all it took to confirm that everything I owned was cheap, nasty and tacky.

'Why can't I get nice stuff like everybody else?' I said angrily, throwing the twins and Nan's presents in the bin. 'Why can't we have money like Aunt Cecilia and Uncle Richard?'

I stayed up late that night playing with my tablet and thinking of what it would be like if we were not so poor. Sometimes, thinking of all the 'what ifs' is not a good thing because I suddenly felt very bitter and resentful. I felt sorry for my poor mum who never had a holiday abroad; for the twins who always have to share one present because Mum and Dad can't afford to mark the occasion twice, and for Dad who works the night shift at the post office because it's an extra 50p per hour … If we had a bit of money Dad could take Mum to Venice, and the twins could have a present each. When you're rich you don't need to wish for things to get better, you just get better things!

I was clenching Galloway's stones so tight in the palm of my hand that I could hear and feel them grind against one another. I was literally holding the power to change things in my hand. All I needed to do was to make a wish and make life better for all of us, change our fate and destiny ... But I remembered that I had made a promise to Geri, and as I don't like breaking promises I reluctantly put the stones back in their pouch, mumbling to myself and cursing at her.

'She won't find anything about the stones because there is nothing to find,' I spat out a bit too loud as I was so angry about the unfair situation. 'It is easy for her to tell me not to wish for anything. She is not the one who has been given a rusty old bike for her birthday! She is an only child and has everything she wants!'

As I was getting angrier and angrier with Geri, I decided to call it a night and go to bed early, wondering what our lives would be like if Mum and Dad had money ...

-8-

'I'm full!' I said, pushing the empty pizza box at the foot of my bed.

Mum and Dad had agreed – after a lot of begging on my part – to let me invite Geri to 'watch a movie for my birthday'. It was the best excuse I had come up with to justify Geri staying late with me that night. She had phoned me first thing on Saturday morning saying that she needed to see me ASAP and that we needed to talk 'face-to-face'; that it was 'extremely important' and that it couldn't be done 'over the phone' in case anyone was 'eavesdropping'. She had been so secretive about what she wanted to talk to me about that you would have thought she had been harbouring an alien and that the FBI, CIA, Interpol and MI5 were after her.

At eight o'clock that evening, Geri turned up on my doorstep with two pizzas, a bag of popcorn, a bottle of fizzy drink and a DVD in her hands. Once again, Geri had thought of everything and I'm sure Mum thought we were going to watch a horror movie and not discuss the biggest secret ever ...

'OK,' she started. 'Now that you've been watered and fed, could I have your attention please?'

'You got it' I said, ready to listen to what she had to say.

'Let's start at the beginning,' she said. 'We know from Tom that Galloway was a druid.'

'Correct.' I nodded approvingly.

'What do you know about druids?' she said sharply. She was pacing up and down my bedroom and I suddenly felt like a witness on a stand with Geri being the defence attorney cross-examining me.

'Not much ...' I said, feeling a bit ashamed about my lack of knowledge on the subject.

'OK, let's start with the basics,' she said rubbing her temples. 'Druids were the priests of the religion of the ancient Celts,' Geri said very matter-of-factly. 'Ancient Celts believed in different gods and goddesses. They believed that nature was sacred and full of spirits. They believed in reincarnation and that the human soul was immortal. They could control the weather; see into the past, present and future. They were magicians, healers, shape-shifters ...'

'Shape-shifters? What are they?' I interrupted her.

'It's when a person transforms into something else, like turning into an animal, for example.'

I was amazed that Geri knew so much about the druids, the Celts and their beliefs. She really had gone out of her way to shed some light on Galloway's stones and I felt a bit bad for being so angry at her the night before, for being so jealous and envious of her.

'Could they really transform into animals?' I asked, sceptically.

'The legend says they could,' she said.

'Ah. Legend ...' I laughed.

'No, Jake. Don't laugh. They are not just legends!' she snapped at me, suddenly very serious. 'We have written accounts of the power of the druids. Famous people like Pliny the Elder, Cicero and even the great Julius Caesar himself have mentioned them and their powers.'

'Really?' I said.

'Yes, really!' she said, rummaging through her bag. 'Look for yourself if you don't believe me,' she added, chucking a thick and heavy looking leather-bound book on my bed. 'I've marked the pages for you. Turn to page 71. Pliny the Elder talks about the ritual of "The oak and the mistletoe" during which, druids would climb an oak tree to cut down the mistletoe with their golden sickle and use the berries to cure infertility. Turn to page 93 now. Cicero talks about druids making predictions and practicing divination: "The druids can tell the future by watching a flight of birds or reading into the entrails of their victims." Page 113 now, Julius Caesar in "The Gallic Wars" mentions the druids building *wicker men*.'

'Wicker men?' I interrupted her.

'Yes,' she said. 'Wicker men. They were large statues made of wicker resembling the effigy of a man used for human sacrifice.'

'Human sacrifice?'

'Apparently, the Celts used to fill those colossal statues with living people and set fire to them to pay tribute to the gods, and the victims would burn to death ... Though, some people dispute Caesar's accounts as propaganda,' she added dismissively.

'I am sorry to ask, but what has it got to do with Galloway's stones?' My head was spinning with all the information I had received in the space of five minutes.

'It has everything to do with Galloway's stones, Jake,' she said. 'You need to understand that druids were not a bunch of old men dressed in white, goofing around. They were powerful people with their own beliefs, their own gods, their own magic ...' she added in a whisper. Her last sentence had sent a shiver down my spine, and I could feel the hair on the back of my neck standing up. 'Where are the stones now?' she suddenly asked.

'Under my pillow.'

'Can I see them?'

'Sure,' I said, rolling on my front and reaching a hand under my pillow to grab the pouch. Geri had put her hands together and cupped her palms in the shape of a little nest like you do when you drink out of a fountain, ready to receive the stones.

'Now, if I am right,' she said, carefully laying the stones in a straight line on my desk, 'the stones should reveal themselves at midnight tonight ...'

'What do you mean?' I asked, a bit confused.

'Do you remember what I told you earlier about the druids and their connection with Mother Nature?'

'Yes, but ...' I started but Geri interrupted me.

'Hear me out,' she said. 'Nature is divided into four elements: fire, earth, air and water ... Galloway was buried with *four* stones ...'

'Do you mean that the stones represent the elements?' I said incredulously.

'Exactly!' she said, pointing at the stones in turn. 'Red for fire ... Green for earth ... White for air ... Blue for water ... Do you know what it means?!' she added with fire in her eyes. 'These stones are more than "wishing stones". These stones have power over the elements!'

If I didn't know any better I would have sworn that Geri had gone mad, that she belonged in a mental asylum, securely fastened in a strait jacket, locked away in a padded room for her own safety. But strange things had happened to me in the last few days; things that I couldn't explain ...

'But there's more,' she continued. 'When I was doing my research I also realised that the zodiac signs are also divided into the four elements: fire, earth, air and water.'

'OK ... I'll have to take your word for it,' I said, cutting her explanation short. I have no interest in astrology and the signs of the zodiac. It's gibberish to me – girly stuff! 'But what has it got to do with Galloway's stones?'

'If I'm right,' she continued, looking at her watch, 'in less than ten minutes we are entering the house of the Gemini ...'

'The house of what?!' I asked.

'Gemini, as in Gemini – the zodiac sign,' she added, as if it was the most obvious thing in the world. 'Signs of fire are Aries, Leo and Sagittarius. Signs of earth are Taurus, Virgo and Capricorn. Signs of air are Gemini, Libra and Aquarius. Signs of Water are Cancer, Scorpio and Pisces.'

I was totally confused, and I think Geri must have realised this because she carried on with her explanation, but a bit slower.

'We're in the constellation of the Taurus for another few minutes, after that, it's the turn of Gemini, sign of air, white stone ...'

'And?'

'And ... *if I'm right*, the power should shift from the green stone to white stone,' she said pointing to the stones with her index finger.

'And what's going to happen?'

'I'm not too sure, Jake ... But we're about to find out ... Three minutes to go,' Geri said, looking at her watch.

We sat on my bed, waiting patiently, as still as two marble statues, not taking our eyes off the stones. The tick-tick-tick of my wall clock seemed to get louder and louder as midnight was getting closer. We heard the church tower strike midnight. We held our breath and it suddenly happened ... It was barely visible at first, like a faint shimmer ... But soon enough, the shimmer turned to a glow... The glow turned to shine ... The shine turned to light ... The white stone was alight, throwing lights like a disco ball onto my walls and my whole room was bathed in a glittery white light. It was beautiful ... We watched the lights spin on my walls for a while in complete silence, not daring to say a word. Then slowly, the lights started to fade away the same way they had come on.

'What's that noise?' Geri suddenly said as the last shimmer of light disappeared.

'Sounds like Dad ...' I said, pricking my ears. 'But it can't be. He's supposed to be at work doing overtime ...'

'It's coming from the garden,' Geri said, opening my window.

'*JOHN?*' I heard Mum say. 'What are you doing here?'

'Celebrating with *hic* my best friend ...' Dad said, holding Mr McDougall – our local drunk – by the shoulders. They were each holding a bottle of beer in their hands, swaying badly, both visibly very drunk.

'Evening *hic* Mrs Fagan,' said Mr McDougall, hiccupping badly and politely tilting his imaginary hat to Mum.

'What's going on, John?' Mum demanded, ignoring Mr McDougall. 'Why aren't you at work?'

'I went *hic* and came back,' said Dad giggling. 'Gave my boss my resignation!'

'You did what?!' exclaimed Mum.

'Don't worry poppet *hic* ... We're millionaires!'

'John, you're drunk and don't know what you're talking about! Come inside now! You're making a scene and you are going to wake the whole neighbourhood up!' Mum ordered.

'Two million, nine hundred and forty-seven thousand *hic* five hundred and thirty-six pounds! You tell her Jim ...' Dad said to Mr McDougall, rocking more and more from side to side.

'Like he said, Mam. Seven and thousand and *hic* hundred

million something or rather ...' mumbled Mr McDougall, before taking another swig of his beer. 'But I know it's short of three million,' he added his index finger in the air as if he had just solved the most difficult mathematical equation ever.

'JOHN! COME INDOORS NOW!!!' Mum bellowed.

At Mum's outburst half the lights in the street had come on and Max started barking like mad. Mr Anderson was hanging out of his window, shouting at us and ordering us all to shut up as it was gone midnight. Dad, who couldn't care less about what was happening around him, was laying on his back, hysterically laughing and making a mud angel. Mr McDougall, who was obviously bursting for a pee, had decided Mum's rose bushes was a good spot to relieve himself against, and worst of all, Geri had witnessed all of it! I was so embarrassed I could have died.

'I've won the lottery!' Dad was shouting, still on his back, moving his arms and legs faster and faster as if he was trying to take off. 'YIPP *hic*! We're RICH!'

'Jake, what have you done?!' Geri suddenly whispered behind me.

'I didn't do anything!' I protested.

'Please tell me you didn't wish for your dad to win the lottery?!'

'No, I didn't! I swear!' I said crossing my heart. My face suddenly felt so hot that I am sure you could have cooked an egg on my cheeks.

'Don't lie to me!' Geri shouted at me.

'I am not lying!' I shouted back. 'I am telling you the truth, Geri. I didn't wish for anything! Last night I might have "wondered" about what would happen if Mum and Dad had a bit more money but I have never wished for anything like that! How was I supposed to know that Dad was going to win the lottery?!' I said, more to myself than anyone else. 'Maybe it has nothing to do with the stones. Maybe Dad just won the lottery fair and square,' I added, trying to reassure myself.

'Give me the stones Jake. We have to destroy them now!' Geri suddenly said.

'Have you gone mad?' I shouted, running to my desk to protect Galloway's stones.

'Jake, please ... Listen to me,' begged Geri. 'We must get rid of the stones. Galloway was buried with them for a reason. The stones must be cursed. Their power is too great, and mankind is too weak.'

'No chance!' I said putting the stones back in their pouch.

'Jake! Think!' Geri implored me 'You've had the stones for more than a week and you could have wished for anything. You could have wished for world peace, a cure to terrible diseases but no – you decided to use them for your own personal gain. Can't you see what is happening, Jake?'

'Oh, I can clearly see what is happening!' I spat back at Geri. 'You are jealous! You want the stones for yourself!'

'Jake, this is madness! We need to get rid of the stones,' she said trying to snatch the pouch out of my hands.

'No!' I shouted at her.

'I can't let you keep them,' Geri said.

'Oh yeah? And what are you going to do?' I said menacingly.

I think I must have scared Geri saying that because she suddenly stopped dead in her tracks.

'You will have to choose, Jake. It's either me or the stones but you can't have both.' She added looking at me straight in the eyes.

'Then I choose the stones!' I shouted at her, holding the stones against my heart.

Geri looked at me for a few seconds, considering her options.

'Fine,' she finally said. 'This will end badly, Jake. I'm telling you. Don't come crying to me when all of this comes crashing down. I've warned you,' she added, grabbing her bag, before slamming my bedroom door behind her.

-9-

For the second time in a month, we had our photo and interview printed on the front of the *Daily Gazette* newspaper. We were all smiling but Dad's smile was the biggest I've ever seen anyone smile. Mind you, wouldn't you smile if you were holding a giant cheque for £2,947,536?

With Dad winning the lottery, our lives were turned upside down once again. It was pretty much the same scenario as when we first discovered Galloway. Random people were shaking our hands in the street, hanging off our fences, phoning to congratulate us, except that this time they all wanted money from us. We received hundreds of letters with funny demands like, 'a tree fell on my car and I need a new one', 'my cat needs a new hip', or my favourite, 'I have made contact with aliens and I need money to build my own spaceship to go and meet them'.

We couldn't go anywhere without being recognised for either having won the lottery or having a Mummy in our back garden. A 'Jake-mania' had swept school, and everybody wanted to be my friend. It's amazing what money can do for your social life. I was suddenly the funniest, coolest, most-handsome kid in school, and I have to admit that I really enjoyed my new status. The only one who was not fazed by it all was Geri. She had not said a word to me since the night Dad had won the lottery. She pretended I didn't exist, and that was fine by me because I didn't need her, especially now I had a whole bunch of exciting new friends. Of course, I felt a bit bad about my behaviour that night and the way I had treated her, but I couldn't explain it or even reason with myself. I had to protect the stones. This was my mission.

Mum and Dad had used some of the money to improve our house and I had trouble recognising it with all the new things that we had bought. We had all the gadgets you could think of; strange and weird things such as a toaster that could poach eggs on the side. I don't know why because we never eat eggs – I guess we bought it just because we could. Brand new furniture and sofas had been delivered and an impressive 70-inch 3D flatscreen TV complete with surround sound system had been installed in the living room.

Mum had had an expensive new kitchen fitted with a double oven, dishwasher, washing machine, tumble dryer and a massive American fridge freezer that produced freshly crushed ice. The twins and I had our bedrooms redecorated and given a wardrobe full of brand-new designer clothes. Dad got Mum a new car, bought a family car and treated himself to a Harley-Davidson motorbike. I finally got a real brand-new BMX and Dad even paid a contractor to finish off the work in the garden. It must have cost a fair bit of money because we now had a hot tub with changing coloured lights, a decking area complete with garden furniture, barbeque and patio heaters and a massive pond full of Japanese koi. Life was sweet and I wouldn't have changed a single thing. We had everything we could have wished for and more. Then one morning, out of nowhere, I felt the dreaded 'snowball' trigger an avalanche ...

'Why don't we go to Florida this summer for our holidays?' Mum said, reading a brochure about America. 'We could rent one of those villas with a swimming pool and a Jacuzzi and visit all the theme parks?'

At the mention of America, the twins had gone into hysterics. They were screaming and shouting and jumping on the spot, throwing their arms in the air.

'I don't know,' Dad said, ignoring the girls. 'Why don't we buy a massive camper van and travel through Scotland? Stop wherever and whenever we want. Go to pubs, do some fishing in the lakes and just watch the world go by ...'

'*John*, how can you even compare sunny Florida in a villa with a swimming pool to a trip in a caravan in rainy Scotland?' Mum snapped.

'Because I can, *Diane* ...' Dad answered sulkily.

Mum and Dad argued all morning about the pros and cons of Florida versus Scotland, with neither of them willing to compromise or budge on their ideal holiday destination. By lunchtime, as no real progress had been made on the holiday front, the twins and I were summoned into the living room.

'This is how we are going to do things from now on,'

Dad started. 'When we have family matters that your Mum and I cannot resolve, we will come here and have a vote. The majority wins. As it is five of us, it will easily be decided. Those in favour of Florida this summer raise your hands.'

Dad had barely finished his sentence and Mum and the twins had already shot their hands in the air.

'And you, Jake?' Dad said.

As it was already three votes in favour of Florida, and that my vote didn't really matter and that I really wanted to go to Florida, I did put my hand in the air too.

'Florida it is,' Dad said shooting a sad look in my direction.

Mum and the twins were ecstatic, and I was left feeling awful knowing that I had upset Dad. Suddenly the prospect of going to Florida was a sad one and I promised to myself not to vote against him ever again. Two days later, I had the opportunity to keep my promise.

Mum and Dad had been arguing about our home. Mum wanted a bigger, better house while Dad was quite happy to stay where we were. So once again we were summoned into the living room and Mum and Dad explained the situation to us. At the mention of moving house, the twins had started crying and had joined the 'stay put' team with Dad. As it was already three votes to one and that I liked our house and that I had promised to myself not to vote against Dad ever again, I had joined the girls and Dad's team. Mum shot a sad look in my direction, and I promised myself not to vote against Mum ever again …

Meeting up and voting in the living room rapidly became a habit. We were voting on everything and anything, from what to have for dinner to what to watch on TV, and since we could never agree and we had money we all started doing our own things. Dad would have his takeaway delivered every night and sit and eat in front of the TV, Mum and the girls would go out for dinner and I was left to my own devices to do pretty much whatever I wanted to do, which wasn't much since the 'Jake-mania' at school was dying off. I realised that I had no real friends, and I was spending most of my spare time on my computer locked in my bedroom, looking through profiles on Social Media. Geri had updated her status, 'Can't wait for Saturday!' She was probably back with Alan and was going to see him play at the weekend. I couldn't say I'd blame her if that was the case as I had been pretty horrible to her …

Our lives became more and more strange and random as the days went by. Dad had bought himself an electric guitar.

'It all brings back memories!' he said, rolling on the carpet as if he was a rock star. 'Maybe I should go back into my music, call the guys, reform the band …'

'Your music was awful back then,' Mum shouted back from the kitchen. 'I doubt very much it has improved since …' she added from under her breath to the lady who was doing her nails and they both started laughing.

I personally didn't think Dad's idea was any more stupid than Mum's, who had decided on a very bright shade of green for her nails.

'What you should do is get a personal trainer, John. You could do with losing a pound ... or two,' she added winking at the nail lady and they both resumed their laughter.

'There is nothing wrong with me!' Dad said, grabbing his beer belly and wobbling it around in such a way that it reminded me of Nan's strawberry trifle at Christmas when she gets it out of the fridge and onto the dining table.

'Mum!' interrupted Samantha. 'Rebecca said I'm not allowed to use her rollerblades even though she is not using them and that they fit me perfectly because I am the same size as her!'

'Don't worry, honey ... Order yourself a pair on the internet,' said Mum, blowing on her nails to make them dry faster. 'Go and get my card from my bag.'

Mum and Dad were far too busy bickering to even care or notice that the twins were turning into real spoiled brats. I was the only one that had not changed. Well, except for the fact that I had to wake up at the crack of dawn every morning to shave my beard, but that was a different matter altogether. Money was slowly tearing us apart instead of bringing us closer.

I had not used Galloway's stones since Dad had won the lottery because I had not needed to, but after a week of constant bickering and tantrum-throwing I couldn't take anymore of Mum and Dad's stupid arguments and decided to take matters into my own hands.

That night as I went to bed I got Galloway's stones from under my pillow and whispered, 'The time has come to for some peace and quiet. I wish for Mum and Dad to stop arguing …'

-10-

Once again, Galloway's stones had granted me what I had wished for; but once again, I had more than I had bargained for. Sure enough, Mum and Dad had finally stopped arguing and instead they were using me as a go-between to pass each other's messages.

'Jake, can you ask your *mother* to pass me the butter, please?' Dad said that morning over breakfast.

'Jake, can you tell your *father* to open his eyes, please? The butter is on his left, within grasp. He simply needs to stretch his arm … If that is not asking too much from him …'

'Jake, can you tell your *mother* it is safer she doesn't touch anything. We wouldn't want her to damage her "lovely" new green nails, would we …?'

After half an hour of 'Jake, can you tell your mother' and 'Jake, can you tell your father', I decided to grab my bag and go to school early. I never thought I'd see the day I would be grateful for school!

As soon as I got back home from school I was greeted by Mum's demands.

'Jake, would you be kind enough to ask your *father* to turn the TV down, please? We can't hear ourselves talk in here.'

The nail lady was back and was now working on Mum's hair.

'Jake!' I heard Dad scream from the living room. 'Could you tell your *mother* to shut the door of the kitchen, please? I can't breathe with the horrible smell of ammonia!'

'Got some homework to do!' I said ignoring them both before running up the stairs to the safety of my bedroom. I had only been back home thirty seconds and I'd already had enough of those two. That night, I decided to make things right and wish for Mum and Dad to leave me out of their arguments!

* * *

'Rebecca, could you please ask your *father* what he has done with the car keys, please?' Mum said, as I came down for breakfast.

'Samantha, could you please remind your *mother* that SHE is the one who used the car last? When she dropped her new "friend" the "talented" beauty therapist back home last night?'

'Rebecca, could you please tell your *father* that MY friend is indeed VERY talented and unlike HIS friend, MINE doesn't spend all her money on drinks!'

'Samantha, could you please tell your *mother* that MY friend Mr McDougall may like a drink or two but that at least he doesn't give me a stupid haircut and charge me a fortune to make me look like a clown!' Dad added, referring to Mum's new hairdo.

Mum's usual long dark curly hair was now short and blonde with some red copper streaks running through it. In all fairness, the new haircut did suit her and made her look younger, but I couldn't help but think that she didn't look like my mum anymore. Once again, the stones had granted me my wish by leaving me out of and Mum and Dad's silly bickering, but it was now the turn of the twins to be used.

As annoying as the twins could sometimes be, I couldn't let them carry the burden on their shoulders. That night as I went to bed, I wished for the girls and I to be left out of Mum and Dad's arguments.

Once again, my wish was granted, and since Mum and Dad didn't have the twins or me to 'pass on' messages, they had resorted to ignoring each other. At first it wasn't too bad because they were simply not talking to each other, which provided some much-deserved peace and quiet, but as the days went by, Mum and Dad's behaviour gradually became worse. For a whole day they ignored each other, pretending the other one was invisible. The day after that, they stayed as far away as they could from each other, as if they were allergic to one another. On the third day, when one entered a room the other one would swiftly leave it. I felt like I was watching one of those theatre plays where different characters enter and leave a room in perfect timing for the amusement of the spectators. Unfortunately for us, there was nothing amusing about Mum and Dad's behaviour, and after three days of constant snubbing I decided to take matters in my own hands once again.

This time, I had carefully planned my wish, as I had learned from my previous mistakes.

'I wish for Mum and Dad to stop arguing and ignoring each other and finally agree on things,' I said to myself, stroking Galloway's stones. 'I think I got everything covered,' I said, happy with myself, putting the stones back under my pillow.

The morning after, I instantly noticed that things had changed and gone back to normal in the Fagan household. Mum and Dad were happily chatting to one another over breakfast. There was no shouting, no arguing – just normal chats. I was so happy with the turn of events, and a huge weight had been lifted off my shoulders.

'Don't be late home from school this afternoon,' Dad said as the twins and I left. 'Your mum and I have something important to tell you,' he added with a wink.

For the first time in a long time, I felt on top of the world. Nothing and no one could have spoiled my good mood, and since I was happy I had decided to apologise to Geri. It is very difficult to get a girl on her own as they are always with their friends. Girls walk in packs and do everything together – they even go to the toilets at the same time! As I was in the queue at the canteen, I suddenly noticed that Geri was a few feet away from her friends, considering what to have for lunch, and I seized this opportunity to talk to her and apologise.

'It's OK, Jake,' she said, after I had said sorry for being such an idiot towards her. 'I'll see you around,' she added coldly, before going back to her friends.

I knew we were never not going to be boyfriend and girlfriend ever again. I was just hoping that maybe one day, we could be friends.

-11-

As soon as the twins and I got back from school, we were summoned into the living room and asked to sit down and listen.

'Last night,' Dad started, 'your mum and I suddenly started talking to each other again. It was the strangest thing, as if a force made us do it. We did not argue and for the first time in ages we finally agreed on something.'

'We need a break from each other, your dad and I,' Mum continued. 'It is nothing either one of us had planned, but after our long chat yesterday everything was suddenly so clear ... The answer was right in front of us. We have decided that it is better for all of us if your dad and I separate.'

Boom ... It was too late ... The avalanche was upon us, leaving us with nowhere to run to ...

'We have already agreed on some terms and conditions,' Dad quickly added before the twins or I could say a word. 'Mum and the twins will go and live temporarily with Aunt Cecilia and Uncle Richard, and Jake will stay here with me.'

'But don't worry,' Mum quickly said before either of the twins or I could say anything. 'We have planned everything. Every two weeks, the girls will go and visit Dad here at weekends and Jake will come down to London every other weekend.'

'Which means, you'll see each other every weekend,' Dad added with a wink as if proud of himself for finding such a 'perfect' arrangement.

'It's for the best,' Mum said with a smile. 'You will thank us one day.'

The whole story felt surreal, as if it was not happening to me but to someone else. I had heard every word that had been said but it was like things were not registering. Of course, I had noticed things had not been great between Mum and Dad – I am not a complete idiot – but I thought it was just a phase they were going through. I had been so absorbed by the stones trying to put things right that I had not seen how bad things had become and where we all had slowly been heading.

That night as I was lying in bed with Galloway's stones in my hands, I started thinking of how I had messed things up for everybody. I didn't want to live with Mum or Dad. I wanted to live with Mum *and* Dad. Of course, I could have used Galloway's stones and made a wish but what if I made things even worse?

'I hate YOU!' I screamed at the stones throwing them against the wall. 'It is all your fault! It's all your fault …' I added before bursting into tears.

✶ ✶ ✶

The week that followed Mum and Dad's announcement went like a flash. I didn't know where everybody was finding the energy to be so proactive, but in less than five days, Mum and the twins had packed the things that they were taking with them to London and divided the rest of their belongings into two piles: one for the things that were going to stay here in Scotland, the other one for what was going to charity. A removal company had been called and the house looked like one of those storage lockers with all the boxes that were stacked on top of each other.

I was the only one not helping with the move since seeing the house being emptied was upsetting me. Everybody was far too busy to notice that I was spending all of my time locked in my bedroom, far away from all the commotion. As the dreaded date of Mum and the twins leaving approached, I felt sicker and sicker in my stomach. I thought a few times of putting things right with the help of Galloway's stones, but I was too scared to unleash another plague on our already fragile family. Each time I had made a wish it had been granted, but each time it had come at a price … Alan, Mrs James, Mum, Dad, the twins – they had all been victims of my wishes. I was the only to be blamed for everything, but no one knew, and each time Mum looked at me and smiled it broke my heart.

On Saturday morning we drove Mum and the twins to Glasgow Prestwick Airport. The twins, who had never been on an airplane, hadn't stopped clucking about their flight to London. Mum was happily telling Dad about her evening plans with Aunt Cecilia and Uncle Richard, who had booked a table at a posh restaurant in Richmond. I was the only one staying silent, looking through the car window feeling sad and upset wishing I would wake up from this bad dream.

As soon as we parked the car, the twins got out screaming with excitement. Mum had gone to check the screen to see if their flight was on time and Dad had got a trolley to put the luggage on. The twins – who can't resist a trolley – had automatically jumped on the sides like they do in the supermarket. Dad was briskly rocking it from side to side to make the girls scream, Mum was skipping alongside them in a fit of laughter and I was left to slowly follow behind the happy party.

At the check-in desk, a quick best-of-three rock-paper-scissor game settled the matter of which twin was going to get the window seat.

'I'll have the window next time,' said Rebecca. 'Mum, can we get some sweets for the flight, please?'

'Yes,' Mum said. 'I need some magazines too ...'

'I'll get them,' said Dad. 'Chocolate and gossip magazines coming up!' he added with a wink, heading towards the newsagent.

The whole experience was surreal. Anyone looking at us now would have thought we were a normal happy family going on a weekend away and not a family about to go their separate ways ...

'I got something for you,' Mum suddenly said to me, handing me an envelope. 'It's your plane ticket for next week.

Your cousin William will be there for the weekend and you boys can catch up. How exciting ...' she added, hugging me close.

I really wished we could have stayed like that forever, but their stupid gate was called and we quickly waved them goodbye and lost them in the crowd going through security.

The trip back home took what felt like forever. Dad was in a very chatty mood and was running me through all the things that 'us boys' were going to do now it was going to be just the two of us.

'We'll go rock climbing tomorrow and tonight we'll have a takeaway delivered and we'll watch some football ... And if we don't feel like washing tomorrow morning then we won't! No one to boss us about!' he added with a laugh.

But the takeaway never materialised ... Nor did the rock climbing or any of Dad's promises. That night, as we were about to order our dinner, Mr McDougall knocked on the door.

'I won't be long, Jake,' Dad said, grabbing his jacket. 'Going for a quick drink down the pub,' he added with a wink. 'Order whatever you want from the Chinese and put it on my tab.'

I never heard Dad come home that night. I only knew he was in because of the loud snoring coming from his bedroom. Dad slept all morning and when he finally woke up at 2 pm he was nursing a serious hangover.

'Turn the TV down please, Jake. I have a headache ...' he said to me as soon as he stepped into the living room. I was watching a programme on the ice caps melting and the only thing you could hear in the background, ever so faintly, was the sound of the whales jumping into the sea. Hardly loud …

'I just got a text from the girls,' he said after making himself a cup of black coffee. 'They went to the National History Museum in London this morning.'

I already knew, as the girls had texted me a good thirty times telling me all about the dinosaur skeletons they had seen.

'How about we go for a nice roast dinner?' Dad said.

Dad and I walked to the Three Bells as it is just round the corner from our house. On the way, we bumped into Alan and Geri. He had his football boots tied by the laces hanging from his neck. I guess Geri must have gone to see him play. Alan simply ignored me as if I was invisible, and Geri waved uncomfortably at me. I waved back, equally uncomfortable, and we all carried on as if nothing had happened.

'Don't worry, lad,' Dad said, patting me hard on the back once Alan and Geri were out of ear shot. 'Plenty more fish in the sea!'

Dad's words of wisdom didn't make me feel any better. Seeing Geri with Alan had upset me far more than I had expected. I didn't blame her for getting back with Alan; after all, I was the one who chose the stones over her. I only had myself to blame. I had made a right mess of everybody's life, and now I had everything I deserved. The old 'reap what you sow' saying was suddenly very meaningful …

As we entered the Three Bells, Dad shouted '*Drinks are*

on me!' The news was greeted by a loud chant of '*JOHNNY! JOHNNY! JOHNNY!*' very similar to the chant at football matches when a striker scores a goal. Dad was treated like royalty down the pub, with everybody patting him on the back, shaking his hand and laughing at his jokes. This reminded me an awful lot of myself at the peak of the 'Jake mania' at school ... Everybody wanted to be my friend then, like everybody wanted to be Dad's friend now. I really wished Dad could see that his popularity was only due to his generosity ...

Mr McDougall and his red nose had joined us at our table halfway through dinner. He may have a bad influence on Dad like Mum had said but I had noticed that he was the only one not taking advantage of Dad and was buying his own drinks.

'How are you, Jake?' he asked me, as Dad had gone to the bar to pay the bill.

'I am OK ...' I lied.

'No need to put a brave face on for me, boy ... I know what it's like. My wife left me years ago and took the kids with her. Haven't seen any of them in more than twenty years ... Sometimes, it's the way things are, Jake. Grown-ups can mess things up ...'

I just wanted to tell Mr McDougall that everything was my fault but before I could say anything he said, 'Don't go blaming yourself for anything, boy. You have done nothing wrong ...'

The truth was far different ... Everything was my fault ...

-12-

Since Dad was spending all his time down the pub, drinking all night and sleeping all day, and Mum wasn't here to get me out of bed in the morning, I stopped going to school. Three days went by without Dad noticing a thing. I reckon I could have got away with not going to school for a whole week if it hadn't been for a phone call from Mr Ryan, my headmaster, asking Dad why I hadn't been at school. Dad, who didn't have the faintest idea of what was going on around the house, looked at me for an answer, and through some complicated mimes and sign language I somehow managed to make Dad understand that I wasn't feeling well.

'Poor lad,' Dad said putting a hand on my forehead to see if I was hot once he had informed Mr Ryan of my lame state. 'It's probably man-flu. Nasty bug that is! There is no known cure for it ... Best thing to do is to lay on the sofa and watch TV ...' he added, passing me the remote control. 'Do you want me to cancel my fishing trip and stay with you?'

'No, it's OK, Dad. You go. I just need a couple of days to get over my cold.'

I felt a bit bad for lying to Dad, but I really couldn't face going to school. There was the happy couple – Alan and Geri

– to put up with; questions about Mum and Dad; getting grilled on the how the twins were settling in London. It was all a bit too much for me, so staying home felt like a much better option ...

But staying home wasn't all it was cracked up to be. The house felt different – eerily cold, silent and empty, as if it had lost its soul. As the days went by, everything and everywhere became a painful reminder of what used to be happier times for all of us. I was missing Mum and the girls terribly, and longing for the silly little things they used to do that annoyed me so much. Like Mum fussing over me or even the twins' stampede up and down the stairs at the crack of dawn on weekends ...

The only place I could just about bear was my bedroom but even all my brand-new stuff could not cheer me up. I would have given anything to have my old bedroom back if that meant we could all be reunited as a family. Yes, I used to hate my cheap nasty brown carpet and my tatty mixed matched furniture, but it was the best bedroom I ever had because I was happy back then.

Everything rapidly became a burden – getting showered and dressed up, tidying after myself, but nothing was more annoying than having to shave my stupid beard every morning. So, one morning, I simply stopped. Dad was away on a 'fishing trip' (pub crawl, more like) with Mr McDougall so there was no danger of him catching me looking like a cave man. I spent a day and a half living like a slob, glued to the TV, hardly leaving the sofa except for toilet breaks and kitchen cupboard food raiding. On Friday evening, as I was engrossed in a repeat episode of an American sitcom, I felt my phone vibrate in my pocket. It was from Geri.

'I'm outside. Open the door.'

Her text had instantly sent me into sheer panic. I couldn't let her in. The house was a complete pigsty. I had tomato sauce stains on my T-shirt and cereal stuck in my beard. I was a complete mess.

'Jake? I know you're in there.' Geri said through the letterbox. 'I can hear the TV.'

'I ... I can't let you in,' I stuttered. 'I'm ill. Very contagious,' I added, hoping this piece of information would discourage her.

'Contagious?' she said. 'Really? Is that the best you can do?' she laughed. 'Come on, let me in. I will not leave until you open the door!'

'Urgh!' I growled through gritted teeth. Girls can be so stubborn and annoying sometimes! 'OK,' I said. 'But you can't make fun of me. Deal?'

'Deal' she said.

True to her word, Geri walked in and didn't comment on my scruffy appearance. Not a word about my filthy tracksuit bottoms and stained top, not even about my beard, which was tucked inside my T-shirt with the sides sticking out like candy floss.

'What happened in here?' she said as she entered the living room, looking at the heaps of pizza boxes, takeaway containers, empty cans and bottles of fizzy drinks, crisps and sweet wrappers, dirty plates and bowls scattered all over the coffee table and floor. 'What's that smell?' she added pinching her nose.

'Curry,' I said, pointing at what was the left from one of my microwave meals on the table.

'No, it's not that ...' she said, looking for the source of the bad smell. 'It smells like ... Dirty feet and BO?' she added, looking disgustingly in my direction. 'Jake ... when was the last time you had a shower?'

Geri sent me upstairs for a shower rather unceremoniously, and by the time I came back down all cleaned and shaven, she had tidied the house, binned all my food containers and opened all the windows to let some fresh air into the house.

'That's much better,' she said with a smile as I entered the living room.

It felt good having Geri here with me. It made me realise how much I had missed her. It also made me realise how horrible I had been to her and for that I really hated myself.

'Geri ... I want to apologise again for everything I have done,' I started. 'Especially for the way I treated you ...'

'It's OK, Jake,' she interrupted me kindly. 'What is done is done. I do believe everything happens for a reason. The good, the bad and everything in between ... Now, what does a girl have to do to be offered a cup of tea?' she added with a smile.

We spoke all afternoon about random things, and it felt that we had never been apart. I told her all about my upcoming weekend in London and she filled me in on the latest school gossip – who had fallen out with who and who was dating who. I was amazed to see how many people can fall out and make up in a week. A lot of names had been mentioned but she had 'conveniently' left out the part about her and Alan getting back together.

'And of course, you and Alan …' I said, trying to sound cool about it.

'Me and Alan?' she said, sounding surprised.

'Yeah, I saw you two last weekend. Don't you remember? You were walking back with him from football …'

'Er … yes,' she started. 'You saw me and Alan walking together. That part is correct. We had just bumped into each other at the top of the road and it felt a bit rude and stupid to ignore him … He was back from his football match and I was back from visiting my Nan.'

'Oh …' I said feeling stupid and relieved at the same time about that piece of news. 'I saw you together and I just …'

'Assumed we were back together?' Geri interrupted me angrily. 'Really? Is that what you thought? Just like that. As if nothing had happened, as if by magic we had travelled back through time and started again from where we had left things?'

'I … I'm sorry …' I said looking at Geri apologetically. But to my biggest surprise she wasn't listening to me. She was frozen on the spot, her mouth still open as if she was yet to finish her sentence.

'Are you OK?' I asked her. She was as white as a sheet, as if she had just seen a ghost.

'Yes …' she murmured. 'I just thought of something …' Geri looked different – distant as if she was somewhere else. 'Jake, could I borrow the stones while you're in London, please?'

'Of course,' I said 'But be careful with what you wish for …'

'I'm not going to make a wish, I can promise you that … I just need to check something …'

-13-

At Heathrow Airport I was welcomed by my Mum, sisters, Aunt Cecilia, Uncle Richard and my cousin William. I never thought I'd say this but I had actually missed the girls and I was glad to see them. It was great to catch up and hear all their stories.

Uncle Richard had organised a day out for all of us in London, and in true Uncle Richard fashion he had meticulously planned everything to the last detail so that we could see and do as much as possible. That is another thing that made me realise how different Uncle Richard and Dad are – Dad always leaves things to the last minute and tends to wing it, and what we end up doing on the day is due to pure luck more than anything else.

From Heathrow, we took a cab all the way to Green Park where we stopped to go to Buckingham Palace and see the changing of the guard. Once we had taken loads of photos of the guards in their red outfits and shiny black shoes, Uncle Richard hailed another cab to take us to Covent Garden where we had lunch on a sunny roof terrace. From where I was sitting, I could see one of those street entertainers down below in the square. He was quite good at juggling, and judging by the money people were giving him I wasn't the only one who enjoyed his performance. It felt a bit surreal to be in London with Mum and the girls. Sitting on a terrace and enjoying lunch felt a million miles away from our old life in Palnure. I suddenly felt homesick and sad at the thought of my poor Dad back in Scotland. Was he down the pub making a spectacle of himself or was he home alone? Whatever Dad was up to was my fault, and I only had myself to blame for splitting up our family ...

After lunch, we took another cab to Westminster Abbey and the Houses of Parliament. I didn't know if it was Uncle Richard's careful planning or pure coincidence, but we arrived just as Big Ben struck two o'clock. A dozen selfies later, we slowly walked across Waterloo Bridge to the London Eye where Uncle Richard had booked us on our own private capsule. I don't do too well with heights, but with that aside, the view from the top of the wheel was incredible. You could see for miles over London's skyline and the people down below looked like tiny busy ants. We finished off the day in Oxford Street where we shopped to death – Mum bought the girls and I loads of smart designer clothes that we didn't need. I was exhausted and couldn't wait to go back to Richmond to Uncle Richard and Aunt Cecilia's house to rest.

I don't know how people work, let alone live, in London. There are noises and lights everywhere and I swear the place never sleeps! I now know what Mum meant when she compared our house to Piccadilly Circus when Galloway was about. I truly enjoyed my day, but I couldn't wait to go back home to Palnure, far away from the hustle and bustle of this mad city life.

The reason why Mum had bought the girls and I all the smart clothes became apparent that very evening. Aunt Cecilia and Uncle Richard were hosting a diner party to celebrate Uncle Richard's 40th birthday. As soon as we arrived we were welcomed by Jenkins the butler, who informed Uncle Richard that everything had been taken care off in our absence. The party planner had decorated the house, the flowers had been delivered and arranged accordingly, the musicians were rehearsing in the conservatory and, finally, the caterer was busy in the kitchen with the final preparations for tonight's dinner.

I felt awkward and uncomfortable all dressed up in my new suit. The stiff winged collar of my shirt kept digging into the back of my neck and I couldn't walk properly in the new leather brogues Mum had bought me. If I felt like a fish out of water in my suit, my cousin William couldn't be more in his element. He oozed confidence, elegance and sophistication. I think he felt a bit sorry for me as he kindly loosened up my collar, straightened my bow tie and whispered a few words of encouragement in my ear.

'Just pretend you belong here. Go and mingle. You'll be fine.'

It was a very posh affair downstairs. Everybody was suited and booted. I don't think I had ever seen so much jewellery in my life. All the ladies were glittering with their diamond rings, earrings, bracelets and necklaces. In the

Victorian conservatory, a quartet of musicians was playing classical music, while a dozen of waiters and waitresses were floating between guests, like weightless ghosts, offering an assortment of canapés and drinks. I was amazed to see how agile they were. If that had been me, I would have already dropped my silver tray and tipped all the glasses on several of the guests.

Mum was in a corner of the conservatory, a glass of champagne in her hand, chatting to a tall thin tanned man in a dark red dinner jacket. I watched them for a while and instantly took a dislike to the man. I didn't like the way he was looking at my mum and I liked the way she was smiling back at him even less.

'Who is the man Mum is talking to?' I asked the twins, who had just entered the conservatory.

'That's Alastair,' Rebecca informed me after a quick glance.

'Who is Alastair?' I asked.

'The divorce lawyer,' said Samantha.

'What divorce lawyer?' I asked taking a canapé a waiter had just offered us in order to be polite.

'Mum and Dad's divorce lawyer, obviously,' the twins said in unison.

'WHAT?!' I said, a bit too loud so everybody looked at me scornfully as if I had just said something very rude.

'Shush,' Rebecca ordered me. 'You are embarrassing us.'

'Why are you so surprised anyway?' Samantha asked me once people had stopped looking at us and resumed their conversation.

'Surely you didn't think Mum and Dad were going to get back together, did you?' said Rebecca.

'Alastair is a friend of Uncle Richard's and a top lawyer in the City,' announced Samantha. 'He has already started the divorce proceedings on Mum's behalf'.

'He is confident this can be rushed through on the grounds of unreasonable behaviour,' Rebecca added as casually as if she had just informed us she liked chocolate.

I instantly felt sick to my stomach at the news of the impending divorce between Mum and Dad. My head was spinning with horrible thoughts of our family being torn apart. I suddenly wanted to be alone, as far away as possible from all those happy pompous people. On the pretence of a drink refill I made my excuses to the girls and quickly ran upstairs to my cousin William's bedroom where I threw myself onto the bed and burst into tears.

I laid there in a flood of tears for more than an hour, and during that time no one came to check on me – not Mum, or even the girls. Why would they? They were having a good time downstairs. They were obviously happy with their new life and didn't need us anymore. Dad and I were now a thing from the past, a distant memory.

Once I had cried and shed all my tears I was left feeling giddy with the worst headache in the world. My temples were thumping hard and I suddenly felt homesick. I wanted to go to our home in Palnure with Mum and Dad and the girls. I would have given anything to go back to our life before the discovery of Galloway's stones, and to go back to what had been happier time. I suddenly realised that Geri had been right all along, and I wondered if poor Galloway had suffered the same fate as me. Did the stones ruin his life too? Did he die alone far from the ones he had once loved and lost to the stones?

After such depressing thoughts, I was not in the mood to rejoin the party, so I got undressed, changed into my pyjama and got into bed. I could hear the happy voices of the guests coming from downstairs, their mood in total contrast to mine. They were as oblivious to my sadness as I was oblivious to their laughter. As I couldn't sleep and I couldn't stand my own company, I grabbed my phone to play one of my games, and to my surprise I had a text from Geri that read, '*Text me as soon as you get this message. We need to talk.*'

If that was possible, I suddenly felt even sicker. I knew Geri had made a wish with Galloway's stones that had some consequences that in time would also ruin her life. I was not in the mood to hear more bad news, so I ignored her text and set my alarm for six o'clock as I had to get up before everybody to get rid of my beard ...

At breakfast everybody was in such a good mood after the party that I didn't need to talk and was simply nodding approvingly every so often. No one had noticed my absence the night before and that suited me fine as I didn't want to have to make up excuses. I kept looking at my watch, counting the hours to my flight. I couldn't wait to go back home to Dad, to what was left of my reality.

Dad was waiting for me at the arrivals. I was so happy to

see him that I ran to him and gave him a big hug.

'Did you miss your old Dad, then?'

'As a matter of fact, I did!' I said cheerfully.

'Well, I missed you too buddy,' Dad said with a smile on his face. 'And, if I may say, I am not the only one who missed you, if you know what I mean,' he added with a wink. 'Geri came to our house twice to see if I had heard from you.'

'Really?' I asked, a bit surprised and weary.

'Yes, really!' Dad answered. 'I told her we should be home by seven. So, come on, let's get going. We don't want to keep your girlfriend waiting!' Dad added with a smile.

- 14 -

Geri was already waiting for me by the time we pulled into our drive. She was sitting on the little wall that separates our front garden from the Andersons'.

'Well, I'll leave you guys to it,' Dad said with a wink. 'I'll be down the Three Bells if you need me,' he whispered in my ear before heading to the pub.

'Why didn't you answer my texts?' Geri asked me as soon as we were alone.

'Because I had an awful weekend in London. The situation is far worse than I originally thought. I found out that my parents are divorcing and I was not in the mood to hear more bad news,' I said looking at my feet.

'More bad news? What are you talking about?' Geri exclaimed. 'Come on,' she added, grabbing me by the elbow and pulling me inside. 'Let's talk in private,' she added, nodding at Mrs Anderson spying on us from behind her curtains.

I was glad to be back in my bedroom among my familiar belongings where I felt safe. I opened my bag and started unpacking.

'What are you doing? Unpacking? We do not have time for

this,' she said, forcing me to sit on my bed. 'I'll get straight to the point. On Friday, you said you thought Alan and I were back together.'

'I already said I was sorry. I ... I just assumed,' I said apologetically.

'Don't worry about that, it's not important,' Geri said dismissively with a wave of her hand. 'But your passing comment gave me an idea, and while you were away I decided to test my theory and I used the stones to make a few wishes.'

'Oh no!' I exclaimed, holding my head in my hands, bracing myself for the impact of more bad news.

'No, it's OK,' she said putting a hand reassuringly on my shoulders. 'Nothing happened. None of my wishes were granted. Do you know what that means? It means the stones belong to you and only you ...' Geri said with a smile.

'And that's a good thing because ...?' I asked sarcastically.

'Because it means that we do not need to worry about the stones falling into the wrong hands. I believe they answer to one person at a time and one person only. Until that person dies that is,' she added very matter of fact before continuing. 'Then the ownership shifts to the next person who gets the stones in their possession. I suspect this is why Galloway was buried with them. He knew their power was too dangerous in the wrong hands and decided to literally take their secret to his grave. He was most likely trying to protect the world from their curse, and credit where it is due, his plan worked for more than two millennia. That is until your dad unearthed Galloway and we sneaked into the tent and found the stones and ... Well, I don't need to remind you what happened after ... But I do believe that you now are the new master of the stones,' she concluded happily.

A couple of months ago, I wouldn't have believed a single word Geri had just spoken. I would have laughed in her face, calling her mad, but somehow I knew that she was telling the truth. Geri said nothing for a while, giving me time to process and make sense of it all.

'Let's just assume for a second that you're right and that the stones do indeed belong to me and that I'm their new master ... Then what?' I asked.

'Do you remember what I said to you after you assumed that Alan and I were back together?' Geri asked me.

'Again, I am sorry. I just assumed you and Alan were back together. I saw you together. What else was I supposed to think?' I said rather annoyed at her for bringing back my mistake.

Geri completely ignored my comment and continued as if nothing had happened.

'I asked you if you thought that Alan and I had started again from where we had left things – *as if by magic, we had travelled back in time.*' She added the last few words in a semi-mysterious whisper that sent shivers down my spine.

'What ... What do you mean?' I said in a stutter, daring not to understand what she had just said.

'I know it is going to sound crazy, but I think our only option is to use the stones to travel back in time and try to fix the mess we've created,' Geri said.

Geri was right. The whole idea was crazy. But it wasn't the craziest thing I had heard or seen and if I was totally honest with myself. For the first time in a very long time, I felt a bit hopeful and had a little glimmer of hope. I even had butterflies in my stomach at the thought of fixing things.

'What do you say?' Geri asked, grabbing my hand.

'I think you might be right. What have we got to lose,' I said, gently squeezing her fingers.

We spent the next three days working out a plan. When I say 'we' I really mean Geri, as I was far too distracted by all sorts of weird events happening around me. Mum's solicitor had sent Dad the divorce papers. Dad had signed them and sent them back without even reading them as he was too busy buying a fishing boat. The twins had called me in tears to say they had been accepted to Wycombe Abbey school (the equivalent of Eton but for girls, they informed me) and were due to start in September. Mum had decided to stay in England and was house-hunting in Richmond with the help of Aunt Cecilia and Uncle Richard while Dad was due to have surgery at a very famous hair transplant clinic in Glasgow. I couldn't help but notice that the madness around us seemed to accelerate at an alarming rate. It was as if our lives were on the brink of explosion, about to shatter into millions of pieces, unleashing the same ashes of destruction onto ourselves as when Mount Vesuvius had engulfed Pompeii …

Geri turned up very early on Thursday morning, which was day four of our 'battle plan', with two takeaway cups of hot chocolate.

'I couldn't sleep last night,' she said as soon as I opened the front door. 'I was up all night thinking,' she continued, handing me over one of the paper cups. 'Something has been bothering me. Each time you've wished for something it was granted to you but never in the way or manner you wanted it or had envisaged it. Take Mrs James for example, or Alan or your beard,' she said, taking a swig of her drink. 'It is as if there is a price to pay for every wish. The stones will grant wishes but at a cost, at the detriment of someone else or something else.'

'The stones are really cursed, aren't they?' I said in a panic. 'We're doomed!'

'Not necessarily,' Geri said calmly. 'Not if we are smarter than them. I think we should go back in time to the day Galloway was moved. That's the morning after your first wish was granted. It is a very important day for several reasons. Firstly, because no one had noticed we had been in the tent. Secondly, because we had the stones in our possession, and we do not need to worry about them falling into the wrong hands. And thirdly, and more importantly,' she added, counting on her fingers, 'none of our lives had gone out of control yet.'

'Then what?' I asked.

'We make sure Galloway goes with Tom to Glasgow and later on that night we bury the stones. It makes sense – bad things only started with your second wish. This is when you inadvertently triggered a series of events leading up to the situation we are in today. I truly believe that if we go back to that key moment then we might have a chance of fixing things.'

'There might be a flaw in your plan,' I started, 'If we go back in time, what is stopping us from making the same decisions we have already made? Think about it … I'll accept Alan's challenge to a fight, I'll ask for the maths test to be cancelled and so on and so forth. It will have the same outcome each time. We'll be stuck in a forever loop where we'll have to relive all these awful events over and over again.'

'Unless …we could *remember everything that has happened to us and learn from our mistakes*,' Geri said, interrupting me. 'It's the only way we can be a step ahead of the stones and beat them at their own game …' she added with a wink.

We spent the rest of the day refining our plan. Geri had made a graph of all the events that had happened in chronological order and the consequences they had had on various people. Her drawing looked like a giant spiderweb that was spinning in all directions, linking and interlocking different people. She had used different colours to highlight the various causes and effects the stones had had on our lives. It was upsetting to see how many people had become casualties to the stones and their curse and how they had all paid a price because of me. I couldn't wait to go back in time and make right the things that I had made wrong.

'That's it!' Geri suddenly exclaimed. 'I think I've cracked it.'

It was now dark outside, and the full moon was glowing bright in the night sending its white milky lights through my bedroom window. Geri had been hard at work for hours on her graph, writing, crossing out and rewriting things. I am pretty sure she was as tired as I was, but she had not complained once and instead had found enough energy to soldier on. I watched her for a while in complete silence and awe.

'Here,' she finally said, handing me over a piece of paper, after another half-hour had passed. 'I think you should read this a few times to memorise it and use the stones to make your wish tonight.'

'Tonight?' I asked surprised.

'Yes, tonight. There is no point in waiting,' Geri said. 'And if I'm right, we should all wake up tomorrow morning a few weeks in the past! Now that is not a sentence you can say every day,' she added with a laugh. 'I'd better go, it's late,' she said, looking at her watch and swallowing a tired yawn.

'Let me walk you home,' I said, grabbing my denim jacket.

Geri and I walked in silence to her house. I felt a bit nauseous, and far too aware of what was at stake. I literally had the power to fix everything for all of us, but I was so worried about messing it up all again. I think Geri must have sensed this because once we had reached her house, she said to me:

'I believe in you, Jake. Just make your wish the same way you have made your previous wishes. You've got this. It's in your hands now. See you tomorrow,' she added, giving me a kiss good night.

On my way back home, some 200 yards ahead of me, I

recognised the familiar shadows of Dad and Mr McDougal. Dad was stumbling pretty bad, having obviously had too much to drink and Mr McDougal was trying his best to prevent him from falling. I ran to catch up with them and give a hand to poor Mr McDougal who seemed to struggle under Dad's weight.

'Thanks, Jake' said Mr McDougal once we had managed to prop Dad up straight and wedged him between us, his arms resting on both our shoulders for support. Dad's breath stank of alcohol, his T-shirt was soaked in beer and he had food stains all over his trousers.

'What happened?' I asked Mr McDougal.

'Stupid landlord, that's what happened!' he said angrily. 'Your Dad was nicely telling the whole pub about how you and him found the Mummy in your back garden that day. He got a bit too excited with his story, started gesticulating and didn't see the waiter behind him bringing food to a table. He knocked the plate over with his pint and the next minute, his glass went flying in the air, spilling its content all over himself and would you believe it, it fell ten feet away, right onto the landlord's new girlfriend's foot and it shattered into pieces! She screamed bloody murder – she was wearing sandals! Anyway, with that, the landlord jumped over the bar like a knight in shining armour to protect his new damsel in distress, didn't realise there was food all over the floor, slipped on it and landed headfirst in a pool of chicken korma, right in front of his new lady friend! What are the odds of that?! He was so furious that he kicked your dad out of the pub, telling him he was barred for life!'

'So, it is the landlord's fault? And it has nothing to do with the fact Dad is drinking a bit too much?!' I asked in disbelief.

'Well, it might have a wee bit of something to do with it, but it's not your dad's fault, Jake,' said Mr McDougal. 'Your dad is a nice person. He's always been kind and he always treated me with respect when other people would make fun of me. Don't think I don't know what people say behind my back. Your dad is not like that. He's a decent bloke who gave me a chance, and thanks to him I'm getting myself sorted. I haven't had a drink in two weeks and for the first time in a very long time I feel great. Your dad is putting a brave face on, but I know how much he misses your mum and the girls. He drinks to forget. Somehow, weird things seem to happen around your family lately and your dad is victim of strange circumstances. I can't explain it ...'

Mr McDougal and I got Dad safely home, but we couldn't manage taking him upstairs to his bedroom, so we laid him across the sofa.

'You go to bed, lad,' said Mr McDougal. 'I'll keep an eye on your old dad.'

I didn't need to be told twice. I ran upstairs in a flood of silent tears. Everything was my fault. I felt so guilty and seeing Dad in such a state had been the last straw. Mr McDougal was right ... Geri was right ... I needed to fix everything, and I needed to fix it now. I got into bed, took the stones from under my pillow and read Geri's notes a few times, out loud first, then silently in my head, slowly falling asleep stroking the stones.

'I wish Geri and I could go back in time to the morning of Galloway's departure. I wish for us to wake up on that very morning, remembering everything that has happened to us since then ...'

I remember falling asleep to the sound of the ocean. I was dreaming that I was on Dad's fishing boat, slowly being rocked to sleep by gentle waves. The wind was lightly blowing the sails, but instead of going forwards the purple boat was going backwards ...

-15-

I was awakened from my dream by a loud noise. It was as if someone was chopping wood with an axe outside my bedroom door.

'Jake! Wake up!' I heard two voices say in unison.

I instantly sat up in bed as if I had been stung by a bee. In front of me, on the threshold of my bedroom, stood the twins.

'Girls! What are you doing here?' I said rubbing my eyes. 'Have you just come back from Uncle Richard and Aunt Cecilia?'

'Uncle Richard and Aunt Cecilia? What are you talking about?' said Rebecca.

'Girls! Is that really you?' I said pinching myself to make sure I wasn't dreaming. Then I suddenly remembered about my beard. 'Don't look at me! I'm hideous! I need to shave!' I shouted to the girls, hiding my face behind my hands but my cheeks were hairless and as smooth as a peach.

'What is the matter with you?' asked Samantha. 'Are you on drugs?' she added suspiciously.

'Oh, my goodness! That is really you!' I shouted in joy, running towards the twins and hugging them close. 'It worked!'

'What has got into you, you weirdo?!' shouted Samantha.

'Get off me!' ordered Rebecca. 'You're hurting me and you're gross!'

'I'm just so happy to see you! I've missed you so much!' I said smiling.

'What? Since last night,' Samantha said sarcastically.

'Never mind' I said, finally letting go off them. 'You wouldn't understand or even believe me! What day is this?' I said, changing the subject.

'Saturday. Why?'

'Oh no! Have they moved Galloway yet?' I said in a panic.

'How do you know he's being moved?' Rebecca said curiously.

'We've only found out a minute ago and were sent to tell you,' Samantha said, eyeing me up and down even more suspiciously.

'Is everybody waiting for me downstairs?' I asked.

'Yes,' said Rebecca. 'Tom and his team ... Mum and Dad and ...'

'And my girlfriend Geri. I know,' I said, finishing her sentence for her before running downstairs.

'That was quick!' I heard Mum's comforting voice say. 'If only you could get out of bed that fast on school days!'

'Mum!' I said running towards her and grabbing her in my arms, lifting her off the ground and spinning her around like a child. 'I love your hair! Never cut it and dye it blonde!'

'There you are!' said Tom, happily. 'You're just in time. We're about to move Galloway.'

'Why?' I asked, putting Mum back down without an explanation to my sudden display of affection. 'Is something wrong?'

'No, everything is fine,' said Tom. 'The equipment we needed to move Galloway turned up unexpectedly this morning. So, it means that we can now move him safely in one piece. The sooner we get him out, the sooner your life can get back to normal,' he added, pointing at a growing crowd hanging off our fences. 'Galloway should be on his way to Glasgow University this evening. Wish us good luck, we're about to start ...'

'No beard this morning?!' I heard the familiar voice of Geri behind me.

'Geri!' I said happily. 'We're back! It worked!'

'I know!' she said smiling. 'How are you feeling?'

'I'm fine. Actually, I'm more than fine. I'm ecstatic!' I said with a huge grin on my face. 'I've got my family back, but I think I'll need to get use to the situation. This sensation of déjà vu feels very weird ... How long have you been here for?' I asked her.

'About an hour ...' she said, looking at her watch. 'I've already checked, and no one knows we've been in the tent, and everything is as I remember it. All that is left for us to do is to make sure the rest of the day runs smoothly. Let's take our front-row seat to the removal of a two-thousand-year-old Mummy ... For the second time!' she added with a laugh.

The afternoon went on exactly as when it had happened the first time. Tom and his team were hard at work. Mum,

Dad, the girls, Geri and I spent a lovely afternoon in the garden, chatting and joking. I couldn't believe how lucky I was to have my family back by my side, to be given a second chance. I had tremendously missed Mum and the girls, but I had also missed my dad and it was good to have my old dad back. I was so happy that I even promised to myself to never get annoyed with the twins ever again – though I meant it, I wasn't too sure how long this would last.

Once Galloway had left, Geri asked me if I was ready to walk her home.

'Do you remember what is going to happen now?' she asked me.

'I do,' I said rolling my eyes.

And sure enough, just as we had reached the phone box down the road, we heard the voice of Alan behind us.

'Hey! Fagan! You little weed!' He looked as angry as I remembered, if not more.

'I'm not interested in fighting you, Alan,' I said before he could say anything else. I think my statement had cut the grass from under his feet because he stood in front of us, mouth wide opened as if frozen in mid-air.

'And for your information, Alan, I'm not your girl!' Geri added with a smile.

Alan was standing speechless in front of us as if he had been disarmed. Our comments had taken him by such surprise that he was trying very hard to think of something witty to reply with but couldn't. A few uncomfortable silent minutes went by before he was finally able to speak. You could almost hear the cogs in his brain ticking, considering his options, pondering his next move.

'Whatever, Fagan' he said through gritted teeth. 'You're not worth the trouble *Mr I've-got-a-Mummy-in-my-back-garden*. You're such a loser,' he added, before gesturing a very rude sign at me and leaving in the opposite direction.

'What has just happened?' I whispered in complete disbelief. 'Has Alan just walked away?'

'Let's calm down and think for a second,' Geri said as soon as Alan was out of earshot. 'Things are slowly falling into place: Galloway has gone, and Alan has gone. Now for part two of our plan. We need to get rid of the stones tonight before their curse strikes again. I think I've found the perfect spot to bury them. I just need to check something,' she added before I could question her. 'Meet me outside mine at midnight. I'll explain everything to you then, I promise. Bring a shovel and don't forget the stones – we need to finish this once and for all.'

* * *

Geri was already waiting for me outside her front door by the time I turned up. She had a bag on her shoulder and a large piece of paper under her arm that looked like a map folded in half.

'Let's go,' she said.

'Where are we going?' I asked her.

'The cemetery,' she simply said, as if it was the most

natural thing in the world.

I couldn't think of anything scarier than going to a cemetery at night, especially during the full moon, so I followed her in silence, too scared to ask what she had in mind. I just prayed it didn't involve digging out an old grave or something. Once we had reached the cemetery, Geri stopped to open her bag and took out a torch and a black object that I recognised as a compass. She had laid the map flat on the ground, and with a torch in one hand and the compass in the other she studied it for a while as if trying to get her bearings.

'This way,' she said, pointing towards Cairnsmore Hill – this I have to admit, to my biggest relief, was the complete opposite direction to the cemetery.

'Do you mind telling me where we're going?' I finally found the courage to ask once we were far away from the churchyard and I was satisfied we were not going to turn into grave robbers.

'To the stone circle' she said.

'Why?' I asked her.

'Do you remember when we visited the site in year four on a day trip with our teacher Mr Brown?'

'Vaguely,' I said. 'That was ages ago. How do you remember stuff like that?'

'I don't know. I just do,' Geri said, shrugging her shoulders. 'Anyway, I remember asking Mr Brown at the time why it was called a "stone circle" when there are only four stones arranged in a square. He told me that there were more stones originally, forming a circle and a cairn stood in its centre, but with time they all had disappeared and now only four of the monolithic stones remained. It is only a couple of miles away from Palnure and I'm pretty sure Galloway would have visited the stone circle during his life. And this got me thinking ... Galloway was buried with four stones ... There are four stones in the circle ... Could this be linked? So, I did my research and stumbled onto something quite interesting. According to different myths and traditions, the four elements are also linked to the four cardinal directions. The north is traditionally linked to the earth element, the south to the fire element, the east to the air element and the west to the water element. And guess what? I've checked on my map and each one of these stones faces a different direction and is aligned perfectly with the cardinal directions. I think it is more than a coincidence. It is a sign and the perfect place to bury the stones.'

Once again, I was amazed by how clever and knowledgeable Geri was. You could tell she had thoroughly done her research and knew what she was talking about. I'm sure she is going to be a great police detective when she's older – with her talent of deduction and attention to detail she's going to rival, if not surpass, the great Sherlock Holmes himself!

'There,' she said, pointing ahead. We had just got out of the woods and right in front of us, in the middle of a clearing, stood the four majestic monolithic stones. I had forgotten how tall they were – at least ten feet – and all had different shapes and forms. There was something eerie, almost mystical, about the place. The giant rocks glistened under the full moon's light as if someone had sprinkled them with magic dust. It was a beautiful spot, and you could see why the ancient people had chosen this site to build their impressive structures. Even though we were alone in the woods in the middle of the night, I wasn't scared anymore. On the contrary, I felt at peace, as if we were meant to be there.

'What do we do now?' I asked Geri in a hushed voice, as I didn't want to break the stillness of the night.

'We split the stones up and bury them separately to break their curse. Together they are too powerful, too dangerous. We cannot risk them falling into the wrong hands once we're gone. We start with this one,' Geri said, pointing at a P-shaped stone. 'It is the north stone according to the compass. Start digging, Jake.'

I did as I was told and started digging a hole right at the foot of the northern stone. I kept digging without complaint, and the more I dug the more it reminded me of the time Dad and I had dug the hole in our garden for Mum's pond which led us to Galloway's discovery and which in turn landed us in the mess we were in.

'That's deep enough. One down. Three more to go,' Geri said once I had reached three feet down. 'To the south stone now,' she said pointing at the monolith in the opposite direction.

I think I must have been digging for a good couple of

hours that night. I was glad when Geri finally said we were done because I felt very hot, sweaty and sticky, and I felt even more glad when she handed me a bottle of water and a chocolate bar that she had packed in her bag. Geri and I sat for a little while on the grass, our backs resting against one of the stones. It was a beautiful night, and the air was soft and the sky was clear and starry. The Big Dipper was right above our heads, and I could see why Dad always said that if you looked at the seven bright stars from a certain angle they looked like a giant saucepan.

'We don't have much time left before daylight,' Geri said, looking at her watch. 'I think it is time for you to make your last wish ...'

'What do you mean?' I asked, a bit startled. 'I'm not making any more wishes. No way!'

'You have to, Jake' Geri said, suddenly very serious. 'The stones have to stay hidden for ever. No one can ever find them or use them ... Ever ...' Geri paused for a few seconds and then said, 'I'm going to give you some time alone with the stones. Just do what you usually do. and when you're done we'll bury the stones one at a time ...' she added, before walking away from the stone circle.

I got the stones out of their pouch and into the palm of my hand. The thought of saying goodbye to them left me with mixed feelings. In one hand I was glad to see the back of them because of the upset they had caused, but on the other they had taught me a valuable lesson and made me more appreciative of the things and people I had taken for granted.

'I wish you stay hidden for ever,' I said, stroking the stones gently. I had forgotten how much I liked the way they felt in my hand – smooth and comforting. 'Goodbye,' I added, before gently closing my fist onto them and slowly making my way to Geri who was waiting for me by the north stone.

'First the north stone. We'll bury the earth stone. The green stone,' Geri said 'After we'll go to the south stone and bury the fire stone. The red stone. Then we'll go to the east stone. The air stone and white stone. And last, the west stone. The blue water stone.'

I did as Geri had instructed and carefully placed each stone at the bottom of their respective holes before burying them again under three feet of soil. If anyone was watching us now, they would probably think I was planting some seeds instead of covering a big secret.

'That's it. That was the last one,' I said, flattening the ground around the east stone with the back of my shovel.

'Then it's time to go,' Geri said, pointing towards the horizon. 'It is almost daylight'.

We slowly walked down the hill, towards the woods, and as we were about to leave the clearing I couldn't resist turning around one last time to look at the stones. And as I did so, I saw four purple sparks rise from the ground and explode mid-air in a grey ash cloud. I couldn't really explain how I knew but I knew that we had broken the curse of Galloway's stones, and for the first time in a very long time I had the feeling that everything was going to be okay ...

THE END